TARGET

BY ALEX WHEELER

SCHOLASTIC INC.

New York Toronto London Auckland Sydney Mexico City New Delhi Hong Kong Buenos Aires

www.starwars.com
www.scholastic.com

ISBN-13: 978-0-545-10612-2
ISBN-10: 0-545-10612-5

12 11 10 9 8 7 6 5 4 3 2 1   9 10 11 12 13 14/0

Book design by Rick DeMonico
Cover illustrations by Randy Martinez
Printed in the U.S.A.
First printing, January 2009

The Emperor closed his eyes and let the rage consume him.

An energy bolt of anger crackled across his body, turning his blood black with venom. A red mist clouded the darkness behind his lids. The fog of hate would have shrouded the vision of a lesser man. But when the Emperor opened his eyes, the blood-tinged world was sharper than ever.

Clarity. Understanding. *Power.*

This was what the rage could do for him. *This* was what pathetic Jedi had never understood, as they rejected their anger, letting cowardice block their path to the dark side. *This* was why they had been eliminated, and why the Emperor reigned supreme, his power unquestioned. His iron rule unassailable.

Until now.

"My Lord, the Death Star has been . . . destroyed."

The Emperor played with his memory of the

moment, polishing it in his mind like a precious gem. Remembering: Darth Vader's voice as he delivered the news. Vader's anger, so forceful the Emperor could feel it from halfway across the galaxy. And with the anger, terror, for Vader knew how terribly he had disappointed his Master.

Vader knew it was not the first time.

The Emperor curled his fingers into a gnarled fist. The Death Star, his most powerful weapon, perhaps the greatest achievement of his reign, the key to destroying the tedious Rebel Alliance once and for all . . . *destroyed*. Even now, the detestable Rebels were no doubt celebrating their victory.

It was a meaningless victory, of course, and only a fool would think differently. But then, only a fool would join the ridiculous battle against the Empire.

Only a fool challenges the inevitable.

The Rebel Alliance was nothing but a nuisance, a millfly to be swatted away.

But even a meaningless victory was unacceptable. The Rebels would be punished. The Emperor smiled — the Rebels would be *crushed*. And soon. His impatience swelled. Fury boiled his blood at the thought of waiting any longer. The rage called for release, and the Emperor knew that with a thought he could destroy his opulent office. He could crack the building's foundation, rain rubble on the heads of those unlucky beings trapped within. He could, with the full power of his anger, unleash a fireball of death.

But he chose to wait. He chose control.

It was another thing the Jedi had never understood. A lesson that even Darth Vader, such a quick study in the school of darkness, had yet to learn. The rage was only a beginning.

Control, that was the key. Patience. The ability to channel the flood, bend it to your will. Anger was the fuel that powered the dark side of the Force. But success depended on *mastery* of the anger. Vader spent his anger without thought; the Emperor hoarded his, as a Hutt hoarded his treasure.

The destruction of the Death Star had been a setback, but every defeat masked an opportunity. And this was an opportunity the Emperor fully intended to seize.

In fact, he already had a plan.

The Emperor activated his comm console, opening a line of communication to the lieutenant who sat quavering just outside the door, waiting on his command.

"Send them in."

Ten of the most powerful men and women in the galaxy faced the Emperor, fear rolling off of them in waves. These were beings who could destroy ships — or cities — with a single word. Their hearts knew no mercy; their lives were founded on cruelties great and small; their names struck terror in their enemies. And yet they trembled before him, made small and weak by their own fear.

The most elite members of his Royal Guard flanked the group, their expressions hidden by their featureless scarlet masks. The Emperor had taken great pains to ensure that his throne room was an awesome and intimidating sight, from the towering walls to the gleaming dais. Behind his shadowed throne, a wall of permaplas windows looked into the heart of the Coruscant night. But his servants ignored the trappings of power. All attention was fixed on the Emperor.

"The Death Star has been destroyed," he informed them, carefully noting their reactions.

Captain Thrawn betrayed no emotion. *Complete control*, the Emperor thought with approval. *This one will go far.* Crix Madine, leader of the elite Storm Commandos, frowned, conflicted emotions swirling deep beneath his surface. The fool thought he could hide his doubts from the Emperor. This foolishness would prove useful, thus the Emperor allowed it. For now.

Commander Grev T'Ran looked somber at the news. But before the expression dropped across his face, the Emperor had sensed something else. The beginnings of a smile. Such a small thing — a tensed muscle, a nearly imperceptible flinch — but it was enough. The Emperor had had his suspicions about T'Ran. Now they were confirmed.

He raised a finger, catching the attention of the Royal Guard. Then nodded. T'Ran's face paled as one of the guards peeled away from the line. His crimson robes swept the floor as he padded silently toward the traitor. The other officers looked away, their faces grim.

"Noooo!" T'Ran drew his blaster. "You can't —"

The guard's force pike jabbed into T'Ran's neck, silencing him forever. His body shuddered once, then dropped to the ground. The silent red figure waited on the Emperor's command, but the Emperor shook his head. They could take out the garbage later. For now, let the traitor stay where he was. It would serve as a helpful reminder.

"How did it happen, sir?" one of the officers asked. "The Death Star was invincible."

"So we were led to believe," the Emperor agreed.

He peered closely at the man who had spoken. His face was blank, his features composed into a perfect mask of calm loyalty. But there was something beneath the surface. Not betrayal, no. But *something* . . . the Emperor reached out with the dark side of the Force, probing the man's depths.

"The Rebels found a *weakness*," the Emperor said, searching for a reaction that would reveal the truth. "Wisely, they exploited it."

Quickly, he ran through what he knew of the man: Rezi Soresh, of the planet Dreizan, a loyal, if plodding commander, his brilliance blunted by blind obedience. Just as the Emperor preferred it. Cold, ambitious, cautious — not the kind of man to speak up first, or at all, when silence would serve him better. And in the Emperor's presence, silence always served better.

"Were there any . . . survivors?" Soresh asked. There was a disturbance in the Force as something flared within him, something sharp and bright.

Hope.

Ah, yes. It made sense now. Rezi Soresh, husband to Ilaani Soresh, father to Kimali Soresh — or was. Two years before, fresh out of the Academy, Kimali had fallen in with a group of Rebel sympathizers. When the group came under suspicion, his mother had helped him evade arrest. She had procured him the text docs he would need to run away and take on a new identity — and then she revealed the truth to Soresh, giving him the chance to say a final farewell to his son.

Soresh had turned them both in. His reward: a promotion to Commander. His family's reward: a life sentence in the Gree Baaker Labor Camp.

Several prisoner work squads had been assigned to the Death Star, the Emperor now remembered. Among them, the prisoners from Gree Baaker.

The Emperor smiled. "*No* survivors."

Soresh's face remained blank as his hope died. The Emperor suspected that Soresh himself was ignorant of the emotions that roiled beneath his surface. Likely, he thought he had left his family — and his guilt — far behind. The Emperor knew better.

"Only Lord Vader escaped," he added, enjoying the disappointment that filled the room. He of course knew of the petty jealousies directed at his most favored subordinate. No one could hope to understand the bond that existed between a Sith Master and his dark apprentice. Darth Vader had failed him before, and would surely fail again, but he remained the Emperor's only option.

True, if there were another — a being with Vader's power and potential, a Jedi with a susceptible mind and a *healthy* body who could rule by his Master's side — Vader would become disposable. But the Jedi were gone forever. He had seen to that.

"Lord Vader is making his way back to Coruscant," the Emperor said. "And when he returns, we will make arrangements to eradicate the Rebel threat once and for all."

"But sir, why wait?" Captain Thrawn asked. "We know the location of the Rebel base. Surely we can —"

"We *can* do many things," the Emperor said coolly, enjoying the way even Thrawn cowered before his glare. "We *will* bide our time. I will not risk generating sympathy for the Rebellion — when it is crushed, it must be crushed *completely*. This does not, however, mean we will do nothing." He pointed a spindly finger at the line of officers. "You will identify the top Rebel leaders. You will use this knowledge to destroy them, thus ensuring that the Alliance begins to crumble from within. And you will discover the name of the pilot responsible for destroying the Death Star." The Emperor savored the rage that burned within him at the thought of it. "The pilot *will* die — and whoever makes this possible will find himself richly rewarded."

Again, he probed the emotions of his officers. Beneath their fear, and their hatred, he sensed loyalty. An eagerness to act. They wanted to please him. But Soresh wanted more than that. He wanted to kill: a bloodlust for the man who had slaughtered his family.

Good, the Emperor thought. Loyalty was useful. Vengeance more so.

The officers filed out, followed by the Red Guard, leaving the Emperor alone with his thoughts. Things were proceeding as they should, he realized now. As they *must*.

He would never doubt the power of the dark side of the Force to show him the way forward. The destruction of the Death Star was surely necessary, as it would guide him to this new path.

Darkness was gathering, and the Emperor sensed that this pilot was at the heart of it. The dark side of the Force had brought him to light. The Emperor had only to find him — and the Emperor *would* find him. He knew that with an iron certainty. The pilot would be found. An ordered galaxy would follow.

It was his destiny.

Luke Skywalker tightened his grip on the lightsaber. Frozen in place, he held his breath, listening.

It was too dark to see, but he could sense *it* out there somewhere, watching him. *Playing* with him. And at any moment —

PING!

Luke sprang backward. The shot screamed past, singeing his cheek. He backed up against a tree, then lashed out with the lightsaber. The blue blade whirled up and around in a smooth, glowing arc. But it sliced through empty air.

PING! PING!

His heart thudding, Luke whipped the lightsaber from side to side, struggling to block the blasts. He was always an instant too late. He took a deep breath and warned himself not to panic.

Use the Force, Luke. He imagined he could hear old

Ben Kenobi advising him, but of course it was only his imagination. Ben was dead. Still, Luke tried to feel the Force. Ben had said it was all around him, that he need only reach for it and it would be there.

Luke reached.

Nothing.

But then: a crackling sound, off to his right. Like a twig being crushed. And something else, a small click. Like a weapon being cocked. Luke lunged to his right, slashing down with the lightsaber in a single, fluid motion. More shots streaked past, and Luke spun around, sweeping the glowing saber from one side to the other, deflecting the spray.

Grinning, Luke raised the lightsaber over his head, ready to deflect the next barrage of fire. But instead of slicing through air, the weapon struck something solid. There was a slow, loud crack. Luke tensed, then — realizing what was about to happen — leaped out of the way.

Too late — again.

The blow came to the back of his head. Luke dropped the lightsaber and went down, slamming hard into the overgrown jungle weeds. A heavy weight landed on top of him, pinning him down. His fingers scraped the ground, searching for the fallen saber, but came up with nothing but dirt.

A soft click, as his assailant readied his weapon.

"Nooo!" Luke screamed. "Don't —"

Direct hit.

"Ow!" Luke complained. It may have been just a sting burst, but a direct hit to the shoulder still *hurt*. He whipped off his blindfold and glared at R2-D2, who came rolling out from behind the tree, looking as pleased with himself as an astromech droid could look. "Artoo, that's not fair!" Luke gestured at the tree branch pinning him flat on his back. "I couldn't block the shot like this, could I? You should have waited for me to get up!"

R2-D2 released a trill of beeps and whistles.

Luke sighed. He'd spent enough time around the droid to guess what he was trying to say. "I know, I know. In a real fight, the enemy wouldn't wait for me to be ready." Not to mention that in a real fight, the enemy would be shooting a blaster, rather than sting bursts — and Luke would be dead.

Now that Luke could see again, he spotted his light-saber lying in a puddle of mud. He stretched out an arm for it, but the weapon was just beyond his reach.

Bring me the lightsaber, he commanded the Force, searching inside himself for the power to move objects with his mind. *Lightsaber.* But the lightsaber stayed where it was. And Luke stayed where he was. Trapped.

"Come on, Artoo," he finally said. "Help me out here."

R2-D2 beeped again, but didn't move.

Luke sighed. The astromech droid may have been his most loyal companion, but he was also more than a little sensitive. "Okay, I'm sorry I said you weren't playing fair," he apologized. "You were just doing what I told you to do. You did a good job."

The droid beeped happily and rolled toward Luke, nudging the lightsaber into his outstretched hand. Soon Luke had sliced away enough of the heavy bough to climb out from under it. He stood up and dusted himself off.

All around him, the lush green jungle rustled and chirped, alive with the calls of woolamanders and whisper birds, gackle bats, klikniks, and the many other species native to Yavin 4. Luke couldn't help feeling like they were all laughing at him.

Better them than Han, he thought, switching off his lightsaber and sliding it back into the holster hanging at his waist. They'd been at the Rebel Base for almost two weeks now — which meant two weeks of fruitless lightsaber practice. And two weeks of being laughed at by Han Solo, who was convinced the lightsaber wasn't good for anything but slicing sweesonberry bread.

Luke knew Han meant well — and that he was probably right about the lightsaber, at least when Luke was the one wielding it. Still, Luke had decided it might be better to practice in the jungle, with no one to watch him but R2-D2 and the towering Massassi trees. He'd need a lot more practice if he was ever going to be a Jedi Master like Ben Kenobi.

Obi-Wan Kenobi, Luke corrected himself. It was still hard to believe that the strange old hermit was actually the last of the great Jedi Knights — and a friend to Luke's father.

I will *find a way to follow in my father's footsteps*, Luke promised himself, resting a hand on his lightsaber. *It's my destiny.*

But at times like this, that seemed impossible. He felt he would never learn to wield his lightsaber with Ben's grace and skill. *And even that wasn't enough for Ben . . . not in the end.*

Luke shook his head, trying to clear it of the images. Ben's lightsaber slashing through the air, sizzling with energy as it clashed against the red beam of Darth Vader's weapon. Ben struggling to match Vader blow for blow — struggling and failing. Ben raising his arms in surrender, meeting Luke's eyes one last time . . . Vader's lightsaber slicing through Ben like he was as insubstantial as air . . . Ben's robes falling to the ground, his body vanished . . . Ben gone.

And Luke alone. Again.

He couldn't stop to think about all he'd lost, or he might never get started again.

His comlink beeped, driving away the dark thoughts.

"Where are you, kid?" Han's familiar voice asked. "Leia's been looking everywhere for you."

Luke grinned, glad there was no one but R2-D2 and a few mucous salamanders around to see how pleased he was to hear that. Ever since he had rescued Leia Organa — okay, since he *and* Han had rescued her — from the Death Star, Luke had felt a special connection to the Alderaan princess. Unfortunately, Han seemed to feel one, too.

"Then why didn't *she* call me?" Luke asked.

"Guess Her Highness has better things to do," Han joked. "Or maybe she's just afraid to get too close when you're waving around that lightsaber."

Luke glared at R2-D2. "How did you know I — ?"

"Blame Threepio," Han said, referring to C-3PO, the protocol droid Luke had acquired back on Tatooine, along with R2-D2. Wherever one went, the other usually followed. Threepio had been more than a little upset that he hadn't been invited along on the jungle training mission. "That bucket of bolts has a bigger mouth than a Whiphid."

"Well, tell Leia you found me, and I'm fine," Luke said, annoyed.

"Tell her yourself, kid," Han said. "General

Dodonna's called some kind of top priority meeting back at Base One — and we're the guests of honor."

Thousands of years earlier, the primitive tribe occupying Yavin 4 had erected several enormous temples across the jungle moon. The largest of these, the Great Temple, was a massive, terraced pyramid whose moss-spotted stone walls broke through the clouds. From the outside, it seemed as ancient and weathered as the moon itself, as if a sacred, mystical secret lay within. But the building had recently been restored and modernized, complete with turbolifts, computers, and lookout posts, as befit the nerve center of the Rebel Alliance.

Luke rode the makeshift turbolift to the top floor. He couldn't believe that only a few weeks before he'd been a farm boy on Tatooine, a nobody stranded in a nothing life. Now he was about to enter a meeting with Jan Dodonna, the leader of the Rebel Alliance military. And why not? Luke was, after all, a hero. With the help of his friends, he'd blown up the Death Star. He'd saved Yavin 4, and possibly the Rebellion itself.

Still, when he stepped into the conference room and saw Dodonna, Han, Leia, and a handful of top Rebel leaders staring back at him, he couldn't help it.

He felt like a clueless kid.

General Dodonna barely waited for Luke to sit down before he began speaking. "Our spies have intercepted a coded Imperial transmission, indicating the Empire has no imminent plans to attack Yavin 4."

"But why?" Leia cut in. "Now that they have our location, it doesn't make sense that they wouldn't attack us."

"Agreed." Dodonna ran a hand through his bushy beard. "We gave them a nasty surprise when we blew up the Death Star, but we didn't expect it would take them this long to regroup. They're planning *something* — but by the time they act, we will have established a new base far from here. I have ships scouring the galaxy for an appropriate location."

"We'd be happy to help in any way we can, general," Leia said.

Han shot her a look. *We?* he mouthed.

The general shook his head. "I'm afraid that's not why I've called you here. We learned something else from the transmission. Although they're not moving on Yavin 4, the Empire *is* determined to retaliate for the blow we struck against the Death Star. They're planning targeted attacks to take out our top leadership — among others. As you can imagine, there's one target the Emperor wants most of all."

As Luke waited for General Dodonna to reveal the target, he suddenly realized that everyone in the room was looking at him. "What?"

"It's you, kid," Han said. "Imperial enemy number one."

"I'm afraid so," General Dodonna confirmed.

Luke wasn't sure whether he should feel proud or terrified.

"According to our sources, the Empire doesn't yet have Luke's name. As of today, we're instituting several new security protocols, designed to shield the identities of anyone who might be an Imperial target," the general explained. "All of your roles in the destruction of the Death Star have been reclassified as top secret. Obviously, your identities are known to most of the Rebels on Yavin 4, but everyone involved understands how crucial secrecy is to the Rebel cause."

"What happens if the Empire finds out?" Luke asked.

"Don't you mean *when* they find out?" Han shot back.

Leia stood up, smacking her hands against the conference table. "Then we face them together, and we defeat them." She sounded almost eager for the chance.

Luke and Han exchanged a glance. Leia was a former

Imperial Senator, a well-known diplomat who — in her official capacity — traveled the galaxy, carrying messages of comfort and peace. But sometimes Luke suspected that deep down, she was the most natural-born warrior of them all.

CHAPTER THREE

When they emerged from Base One, Chewbacca and the droids were waiting. "Come on, Chewie," Han said, barely pausing to collect the Wookiee. "Let's go."

"Go where?" Luke asked, hurrying after them.

"Where do you think?" Han asked, sounding surprised by the question. "I'm taking myself and my ship —"

Chewbacca roared indignantly.

"Of course, you, too, Chewie. What, you think I'd leave my copilot here to get blasted to bits when the Empire shows up? We'll jump into hyperspace and be halfway across the galaxy by dinnertime." Han stopped and turned to Luke, jabbing him in the chest. "And if you're smart, kid, you'll come along for the ride. I've got to admit, you're not a half bad pilot. A few sloppy habits, but you could come in handy once we get a little training into you. . . ."

"Not half bad?" Luke repeated. "I could fly better than you blindfolded and with one arm tied behind my back!"

Han just laughed. "Kid, I was outflying wannabe spice smugglers on the Kessel Run at point five light-speed back when you were still picking up Bantha droppings on Tatooine."

"I was a good enough pilot to destroy the Death Star," Luke pointed out.

"Lucky shot," Han said. "Happens to the best of us — and the rest of us."

Luke fell silent. He knew Han was just teasing . . . but he'd managed to hit on Luke's greatest fear. Maybe he'd been meant to make that shot — maybe the Force had steered him toward his destiny, just like Obi-Wan had predicted.

Or maybe it was just dumb luck.

"Luke may be inexperienced," Leia admitted.

"Inexperienced?" Luke repeated in disbelief. So even Leia didn't believe in him?

"But at least he's not running away." Leia glared at Han, daring him to argue.

"Who said anything about running away?" he countered.

Chewbacca barked again, giving Han a pointed look.

"Hey, there's a *difference*," Han insisted. "I never said I'd be sticking around forever, did I? There's no money to be made here — and if I don't pay Jabba back soon, I'm dead. But that does *not* mean I'm running away, Your Worshipfulness. Only cowards run away."

Leia looked skeptical. "So what would you call it?"

"I'd call it being smart."

"You?" Leia smirked. "Smart?"

Han ignored her bait. He turned to Luke, serious for once. "Look, kid, you heard the general in there. The Empire's gunning for you. Only thing to do now is disappear."

"The Empire's gunning for a mystery man," Luke pointed out. "No one knows that I'm the pilot they're looking for."

Han threw up his arms in disgust. "Kid, look around — everyone on this whole moon knows."

"The new security protocols will take care of that," Leia pointed out.

"You trust security protocols if you want," Han said. "I trust my gut. And my gut says when this many people know a secret, it won't be a secret for long."

"Master Luke, I'm inclined to agree with Captain Solo," C-3PO put in, sounding agitated. "When you say that the Empire is *gunning* for you . . . well, that sounds like a situation that could end rather unhappily, don't you think? Perhaps we'd be safer somewhere else, away from all this troublesome fighting."

R2-D2 let off a long string of beeps.

C-3PO looked infuriated. "That's all well and good for you to say," he told the droid, "but some of us are designed for dignified intergalactic summit negotiations, not —" his voice took on a disgusted note " — *space battles*. I am, after all, a protocol droid fluent in over six million forms of communication and equipped with —"

"We know, Threepio," Luke said wearily. The droid gave some version of this speech at least once a day. "And I'm sorry I got you mixed up in this. But we're in it now. And I'm not running away, no matter how dangerous it may be. I'm a Rebel, and I'm going to stick around and fight."

That's what a Jedi would do, right, Ben? he thought. But of course there was no answer. At two crucial moments, he'd thought he heard Ben speak to him from beyond the grave. But it had never happened since.

Luke was beginning to think it may just have been his imagination.

"You see? Luke's not afraid," Leia said proudly.

Luke grinned.

"Running away from the guy with the blaster pointed at your head isn't fear, Your Highness," Han retorted. "It's smarts. Or did they not teach you that in princess school?"

"I guess they were too busy teaching us the importance of fighting for what you believe in, even when the cause seems hopeless," Leia snapped. "Or did they not teach you that in smuggler school?"

"They taught me how to stay alive, princess. And that's all I'm trying to teach you."

"Oh, my, how lucky I am to have met you!" Leia gushed, affecting a high, fluttery voice. "I don't know how I managed to make it this long without having a big, strong man like you around to keep me safe."

Han shrugged. "You said it, princess, not me."

"Come on, Han," Luke urged him. "The Rebellion could really use you."

"I won't be any good to the Rebellion if I'm dead," Han said. "And neither will you. We lift off in a few hours — you want to join us, you're welcome. You want to stick around here? Well . . . it's been nice knowing you, kid. You, too, princess," he told Leia. He held out a hand for her to shake.

She crossed her arms.

Han snorted. "Have it your way. C'mon, Chewie."

The Wookiee groaned a mournful goodbye as he followed Han to the main hangar deck.

"You don't think he'll really leave, do you?" Luke asked, once they were gone. Han might be annoying sometimes, but he was still a good pilot — and a good friend.

Luke didn't have many of those left.

"I hope he does," Leia said angrily. "The sooner, the better."

But Luke suspected she didn't mean it. Judging from the look on her face, she wanted Han to stick around as much as he did.

Maybe more.

"You don't think he's right, do you?" Luke asked nervously.

"Not a chance."

"There is, in fact, a ninety-four point two percent chance that Captain Solo is correct," C-3PO pointed out. "Especially if you factor in —"

"Not a chance," Leia repeated firmly. "I believe in the Alliance. We *will* protect you, Luke. And, you know, I also believe in you."

"You do?" Luke asked, flushing with pleasure.

"Of course," Leia said, like it should have been obvious. "You've already proven you can stand up to the Empire and survive. The Death Star was the most powerful weapon they had. What could be worse than facing that?"

Luke shuddered. "Let's hope we never have to find out."

*   *   *

Commander Rezi Soresh had been waiting a long time for an opportunity like this. He knew what everyone thought of him. That he was all brain, no guts. That he was quick to obey but slow to initiate. He knew they laughed at him, as people had always laughed — and so they would pay, as people always paid. Even Ilaani had laughed at him, as if she —

No, he thought. He would not think of the traitor or her son. Not at a time like this. He had work to do. This new mission was his chance to prove himself to the Emperor, once and for all. Once he stood by the great man's side, there would be no more laughter.

None of the Emperor's officers could match Rezi's ambition, his intelligence, his determination. And certainly none could match his loyalty. The Emperor's goals were his goals; the Emperor's desires, his desires; the Emperor's will, his will. The Empire was his life.

And he had proven that like no one else.

Now he would prove it again, so thoroughly and so impressively that no one, not even the Emperor, would be able to ignore him. And no one would be able to laugh.

The comlink beeped with an incoming transmission. Soresh put it up on the viewscreen.

Hollow gray eyes stared out at him, deep set in a pale, angular face. The shaved head had been replaced by a shock of black hair, which made the man look more human.

Looks could be deceiving.

The man didn't speak. He merely waited for orders; he'd been well-trained.

"I have a job for you," Soresh said.

The man nodded, still waiting.

"It's too sensitive to discuss over a comm channel," Soresh told him. "How quickly can you get to Coruscant?"

"I have something to finish here," the man said. "Then I'll have to track down a ship." His voice was empty of emotion. Like his face, it was blank, almost machine-like. As if he were a droid pretending to be human, and doing a poor job of it. But Soresh, who knew him better than anyone, knew there were no mechanical parts hiding beneath the surface.

Beneath the surface there was . . . nothing. He sounded hollow because he was. Soresh knew this — he'd made sure of it.

"I can be there in three days," the man said.

"Make it one." Soresh flipped off the comlink without waiting for an answer. He knew the man would obey. Soon he would arrive on Coruscant, and then Soresh would sic the hunter on his prey.

At the thought of it, an odd shiver of foreboding ran

up his spine. There was no reason for concern. It was a foolproof plan, guaranteed to work. And yet . . .

He had the dark feeling that he had just sealed his own doom. The man with the hollow eyes was trained to kill — he knew nothing else but the joy of the hunt. And soon he would have the pilot who'd destroyed the Death Star in his blaster sight. So why did Soresh feel he'd just signed his own death warrant?

So be it, he thought, imagining his inner voice traveling across the dark emptiness of the galaxy and whispering in the pilot's ear. *Then you and I shall die together.*

CHAPTER FOUR

We are nothing," he repeats, as he is told. The light blinds him. He opens his eyes wide against the pain. "We are no one."

"You belong to me," the Commander says.

"We belong to you."

They are seven. But they are one.

One in mind. One in obedience. One in life.

They are no one.

"Count off," the Commander says.

The young men obey. "X-1!" shouts the first. "X-2!" the second. And down the line.

He waits. And then, "X-7!" he shouts.

The lights blink out. Darkness.

"Time to sleep," the Commander says.

X-7 braces for the blow. It is always sooner than he expects, always harder. Pain blossoms from the back of his head, blots out the world.

Time to sleep.

*   *   *

Once he'd plotted the course to Coruscant, X-7 stretched out on his bunk, staring at the ceiling. The Preybird starfighter had seen better days, and it wasn't much for comfort or show, but the auto-pilot would take him where he needed to go. At least, that's what the Rodian had boasted, before he died.

No need to go anywhere now, my friend, X-7 had told the Rodian lying lifeless at his feet. *So I'm sure you won't mind if I take her for a spin.* Then he'd holstered the blaster and lifted off.

The Commander wanted him on Coruscant within a day. And what the Commander wanted, the Commander received.

For X-7, these were words to live by.

Literally.

The stun cuffs pin him against the durasteel wall. The light pierces his eyeballs, and the figure facing him is nothing more than a shadow.

But he knows it is the Commander. It is always the Commander.

He does not struggle. He only waits for this moment

to pass, and then the next. He dreads the future; the past is forbidden. The present is his only home.

"Who are you?" the Commander asks.

"I am X-7."

"What is your purpose?" the Commander asks.

"To serve you."

"To what end?" the Commander asks.

"To serve the Empire."

"Where do you come from?" the Commander asks.

"From nowhere."

Pain. Everywhere at once. It is born inside of him, exploding out of him, and then it is gone.

"Where do you come from?" the Commander asks again.

"I cannot remember." He gives the answer the Commander wants to hear.

Pain. Greater now, more intense, like a knife hollowing him out.

"Liar!" the Commander roars. "Have you not yet learned it is impossible to lie to me?"

The sensors on his forehead take measure of his thoughts, his emotions. He has no secrets from the Commander. He has no secrets.

"What do you remember of your past?" the Commander presses him.

"Nothing," he gasps, already anticipating the pain

that follows in the next instant. The explosion in his brain casts a shadow of darkness, and for a blissful moment, he is lost. But the Commander calls him back, jolts him awake.

He wants to obey. He wants to blot out his memories, to empty himself of the past. He struggles to erase it all.

He has no name. No history. His life is blank. He remembers nothing but these walls, the light, the Commander's voice. Pain. Almost nothing . . . but.

There are images. A small girl, blond, with an innocent smile. A grassy hill, and just beyond it, a lake, cool and refreshing. Two suns blazing against a violet sky. A woman's voice. A hand on his forehead, soft and warm. He wants to forget . . . but not as much as he wants to remember.

They are only images; they are all he has left.

"Tell me what you remember," the Commander says. His finger twitches over the switch that will bring the pain.

He would rather die than survive another jolt. And they will not let him die.

"I remember . . . a girl," he says softly. "She is my . . ." Sister? Friend? Daughter? But the memory will not come. Only her face. Only her smile. "She is mine," he tells the Commander.

The Commander smiles. "Not anymore."

*　　*　　*

The hours crept by as X-7 drew closer and closer to Coruscant. X-7 knew, because he had done extensive research on "ordinary" behavior, that most beings would feel the need to fill the time. They would fiddle with a datapad, play a game of dejarik, even gaze out the window at the emptiness of space. And when necessary, X-7 would do the same. On a mission, he was well-equipped to fit in.

But alone, he had no such need. He had stripped the mattress from his bunk. The rigid durasteel against his back felt comfortably familiar. He appreciated these hours, alone in space. So much of his life was a careful act. Isolated moments like this came as a relief. He could drop the mask and exist as he was: empty.

No one in the galaxy had ever seen X-7 like this, his true self exposed. No one but the Commander, of course, who knew him inside and out.

As he should: the Commander had made him.

He faces the Commander as an equal, though they will never be equals. There are no more restraints, no more sensors, no more neuronic binders to inflict punishing pain. They are well beyond this. He sits on one side of the desk, the Commander on the other. He waits.

"Congratulations, X-7," the Commander says. He holds out a hand, and X-7 knows to shake it. He has been well-trained. He can act human.

The Commander tells him he is human.

The Commander tells him that the lessons he's learned — how to smile, how to laugh, how to imitate sorrow or fear or joy — are things he used to understand instinctively. That he once was a being like other beings, soft and stupid.

He feels sorry for that other self.

He is grateful to the Commander for eliminating it.

"I have to admit, I always thought X-3 would be the one," the Commander says, shaking his head. "He seemed somehow . . . impervious."

But he had not been impervious to X-7's vibroblade in their final training bout.

X-1 and X-6 had been easily dispatched. X-2 had malfunctioned, tried to escape. X-5 had malfunctioned as well, begun muttering about alliances, encouraged the others to see the Commander as their enemy. That was before X-7's emotions had died away — he had been able to enjoy the kill. X-4 hung himself with a laser whip.

And then there was one.

"*They were your friends, once,*" the Commander says. "*Your partners in our exciting new venture. You feel no sorrow over their deaths?*"

He knows the Commander is testing him, but they are beyond tests now. He feels no anxiety — he has nothing to hide.

"*I feel nothing,*" he says honestly, "*but the desire to obey.*"

The Commander nods. "You're ready. There's just one last thing. I want to introduce you to someone." He presses a button on his console, and a screen rises from the desk.

A face appears.

His head is shaved. Young, barely more than a child, but with the eyes of a man, stone gray and cruel. His thin lips are pressed together, a flat line running parallel to the single crease in his forehead. His skin is purpled with fading bruises, and a network of thin scars spiders across his scalp. "Recognize him?" the Commander asks.

X-7 shakes his head.

The man on the screen shakes his head.

X-7 opens his mouth to speak.

The man on the screen opens his mouth to speak.

X-7 understands.

The Commander sees it in his eyes, presses a button,

and the mirrored screen drops back into the desk. X-7
realizes this was the final test.

He has passed.

He is ready.

Since X-7's last trip to Coruscant, the Commander
had switched offices. He was now located midway up
a towering spire in the planet's wealthiest quadrant.
But this office was identical to the other, lacking in
any personal effects. The spare space contained only a
desk, a single shelf, and a wall-sized viewscreen.

"Welcome," the Commander said, gesturing for X-7
to take a seat.

There had been a time when the Commander had
been the only being he knew. His face had filled
X-7's world. Now, many missions later, after traveling
the galaxy and encountering beings of all kinds, X-7
understood that the Commander was unusually thin
and weak. His watery eyes, his pinched features, his
stooped shoulders — they were not the mark of an
intimidating man.

X-7 saw all this objectively, as he saw everything
objectively. He saw the being before him as others saw
him. *Rezi Soresh*, he thought, testing the name in his
mind, trying to fit it to the man.

But it was no use. The man before him would always

be the Commander, the center of his universe. Pleasing the Commander was all he needed in life; disappointing the Commander was death. He understood now that this was not natural. This was not the way other beings lived. Other beings had desires of their own, names, identities, histories. X-7 had no name, only a designation, like a droid. Other men had free will, while X-7 had only Soresh.

He knew this to be true, and he knew that Soresh had done this to him. But knowing the truth changed nothing.

X-7 had free will as well — and, like all other beings, he willed himself to be happy.

Happiness was obeying Soresh.

The Commander passed a datapad across the desk. "A valuable piece of Imperial property has been destroyed by the Rebel scourge. Your target is the pilot who fired the fatal blow. You will infiltrate the Rebel Alliance, gain proof of his identity, and report back. The datapad contains everything we've got on the Alliance. Operations, security protocols, personnel data — everything."

X-7 nodded.

"You will arrange to be in a position to kill him, on my command," the Commander continued. "You will cast the blame on someone else, so that *you* can remain at the heart of the Alliance. Everything they know, you will know. And everything you know, I will know."

"For how long?" X-7 asked.

The Commander smiled. "Until the pilot is dead and the Rebel threat has been eliminated."

X-7 rose, tucking the datapad securely into his utility pouch. "It will be done."

CHAPTER FIVE

The situation is more dire than even you know, princess," General Dodonna said, his expression sorrowful.

When the general requested a walk through the lush temple grounds, Leia had expected nothing more than an evening of polite conversation. But the general obviously had more serious concerns on his mind — concerns that he preferred to keep between the two of them.

"A substantial portion of the Rebellion's funds were located on Alderaan," the general said.

Leia flinched at the name of her home planet. Just hearing the word sent a shockwave through her. Beautiful, peaceful Alderaan, blasted into a billion pieces of space rubble. Every being on the planet ground to dust. Millions of lives lost in a heartbeat.

In *her* heartbeat, as she stood on the bridge of the

Death Star, helpless to stop it. There was nothing she could have done, she knew that.

And yet she still hated herself for it. For doing nothing — while her planet, her past, her own *father*, were lost forever.

She forced the memories back inside herself, not wanting to reveal her weakness to General Dodonna.

"The funds, along with several key financial access codes, were lost with the destruction of the planet," the general continued. "We find ourselves in dire straits. Of course, the Rebellion lives and breathes through the sacrifices of its brave fighters, but . . ." He sighed. "I'm afraid we must not lose sight of the more practical concerns. Without sufficient funding, we'll have no ships, no weapons, no defenses, and no hope of establishing a new base."

"*All* the funds were housed on Alderaan?" Leia asked, surprised that the Rebellion leadership would have been so foolhardy.

The general shook his head. "This is why I wanted to speak with you. We have a set of secret accounts on the planet Muunilinst."

Leia started in surprise. Although the InterGalactic Banking Clan had been disbanded, Muunilinst, its former home, was still the financial heart of the galaxy. *And* an Imperial stronghold. Thanks to their financial skills, the Muuns were one of the few alien species actually tolerated — and even respected — by the Empire. But Leia knew there was still a strong Imperial presence on the planet.

"It will be dangerous to retrieve the funds," General Dodonna admitted. "But it must be done. Our contact on the planet, Mak Luunim, is holding a datacard containing the access codes. Once you've retrieved them, he's agreed to help you transfer the accounts offworld and get you safely off the planet."

"Get *me* safely off the planet?"

"You're the only one I trust for a mission like this, princess."

Not so long ago, in what seemed like another life, Leia had preferred to be addressed by her other title, senator. Proud as she was of her royal birthright, she was even prouder of the hard work and determination that had gained her a seat in the Galactic Senate. Now, however, the titles seemed interchangeable. The Senate had been; Alderaan was gone. And the person she'd been — the peace-loving princess, the silver-tongued senator — that was gone, too.

"General Rieekan's expecting me on Delaya, in the Alderaan system," Leia reminded him. A group of Alderaan survivors — beings who had been offworld when the Death Star attacked — had begun to assemble there. Leia was eager to join them. She had told General Dodonna that she hoped the survivors might agree to join the Alliance — and this was true. But she also felt a deep need to be with her people, and not just because she was their leader.

They were all she had left of her homeworld. They needed her — but she needed them just as much.

"If all goes well, this should be an easy mission, in and out," the general said. "You can go directly from Muunilinst to Delaya. That is, if you're willing."

"Of course, general." This was the only possible response. Whatever the Alliance asked of her, Leia would give.

"Excellent. I've already arranged transportation — you'll leave tomorrow evening. Mak Luunim is expecting you. And Luke."

"Luke?"

"I thought it might be best for him to accompany you. He's certainly proven himself as willing and able to assist the cause."

And you want him off Yavin 4, in case the Empire comes looking for him, Leia thought. But she couldn't disagree — and she would be glad to have Luke with her. It would have felt wrong to leave him behind.

Why is that? she asked herself. She barely knew Luke, and yet in the short time they'd been together, he had come to be important to her. More than that, he seemed almost a part of her. *And he's not the only one*, she thought. Han's infuriating grin flashed across her mind.

Leia shook her head, trying to brush away the image.

Focus on the Rebellion, she reminded herself. *Nothing else matters.*

"I won't let you down, general," she assured him.

"You never do." He rested a hand on her shoulder, favoring her with a smile. Leia stiffened, suddenly reminded of her father. She had lived for the moments he'd smiled at her like that, loving and proud.

She would never see that smile again.

Once Leia briefed Luke on the mission, they headed to the spaceport. It was always a good idea to rendezvous with the pilot before a mission, especially since they only had one day to formulate a strategy and assemble supplies. As they approached the hangar deck, Leia spotted Chewbacca wheeling a cart of lubricant hoses toward the *Millennium Falcon*. As always, the dilapidated Corellian freighter appeared to be held together with tape and good luck — but Leia knew from experience that it was tougher than it looked.

Han, leaning against the *Falcon*'s aft hull, offered them a jaunty wave.

"What are you still doing here?" Leia asked sourly.

"Waiting for my passengers." Han flashed that incredibly annoying smirk of his. "Don't worry, once Chewie finishes tweaking the hyperdrive, he'll lay out a banquet fit for a princess. I know how you royal folks like to travel in luxury."

Chewie let out a long, warbling whine.

Han rolled his eyes. "I *know* food service isn't part of your job description, you furry oaf." He leaned toward Leia and lowered his voice to a loud whisper. "That's the problem with Wookiees — can't take a joke."

As Chewie roared in protest, Leia forced herself not to smile. She knew Han was just trying to get a reaction out of her, and she wasn't about to comply. "What makes you think I'm going anywhere with you?"

Han shrugged. "No one's forcing you, Highness. If you changed your mind about going to Muunilinst, that's your business."

Luke's eyes widened. "*You're* our transportation to Muunilinst?"

Han gave him a mock salute. "At your service."

"Thanks but no thanks, flyboy." Leia shook her head. "This isn't your fight, remember? I'm sure you have better things to do — on the other side of the galaxy."

For a second, Han looked wounded. Leia felt guilty. She didn't *mean* to say things like that to him — they just popped out whenever he was around. If only he wasn't so *infuriating*. There was just something about him. She often wished she'd never met him — but deep down, a rebellious part of her didn't want him out of her sight.

Han scowled. "Look, Your Worship, you know this bird's the fastest and fiercest in the galaxy. You want to get somewhere, the *Millennium Falcon*'s the way to go."

"And what's in it for you?" Leia asked suspiciously.

"Nothing," Han said.

Chewbacca yowled, and Han shot him an annoyed glare. "Okay, fine, so there's a little something in it for me, but it's barely enough to pay for the fuel. Then I'll drop you two on Delaya, and you never have to see me again."

"I knew it!" Luke said, sounding overjoyed. "You can talk all you want about walking away from the Rebellion, but when it comes right down to it, you're on our side."

"Hey, slow down," Han protested. "I'm just flying you from point A to point B. Trust me, it's not because I'm joining your nutso Rebellion."

Luke shook his head. "Say what you want, but I know you believe in this fight and want to help."

Leia looked at Luke in amazement. He sounded so sure. Like he could look straight through Han and see the truth of his soul. Leia wondered what it would be like to be so certain about people — to look at them without doubt or suspicion. Some might call Luke naive, but there was something bold in his willingness to trust his instincts.

Even when they were wrong.

"I appreciate the vote of confidence, but you've got me figured all wrong," Han said, sounding almost sorry.

"I'm not wrong." There was an unusually steely note in Luke's voice, different from his usual young, questioning tone. "I know you, Han. I can see the good in you, even if you can't."

"Not everyone has a good side, kid. Not everyone's like you." Han glanced at Leia. They were alike in this, she realized — both of them saw the danger in Luke's willingness to trust. And maybe both of them envied it. "The sooner you figure that out, the longer you stay alive."

e would begin with Leia.

X-7 had no doubts about his plan. Princess Leia Organa was the public face of the Rebellion, but the Empire's informants suggested she was more than that. She was a key decision-maker, a diplomat, a leader — she would know the name of the pilot who destroyed the Death Star. And she would have access to him.

As the Preybird hurtled toward the Rebel Base, X-7 skimmed the datapad, soaking in every piece of information that existed on Leia Organa. His training had given him the ability to read and memorize information with great speed, and soon he had become an expert on the Alderaan princess. Everything the Empire knew about Leia, X-7 knew.

He knew what she liked and what she hated. What she respected. *Whom* she respected.

And that was the person he would become.

*   *   *

Yavin 4 loomed in the viewscreen, the jungle moon awash in swirls of blue and green.

The comm console lit up with an incoming transmission. "You are entering restricted territory," the scratchy voice warned.

"Request clearance for landing."

The replay came as expected. "Landing code required."

X-7 recited the code he'd been given by the Commander, and armed his laser cannons. He'd been assured that the Rebel codes were only a few months old, and that the spy who'd delivered them could be trusted. Still, he believed in being prepared.

"Permission granted. You may land when ready."

X-7 smiled. Not because he was happy, but because expressing the emotion he couldn't feel was good practice. Soon he would be one of them.

"Nice and slow," the man said, cocking his blaster as X-7 stepped through the hatch of the Preybird. "And let's keep your hands where I can see them."

So they hadn't been fooled by the landing code after all. *Smart*, X-7 thought in approval. Allowing him to land and let his guard down before revealing themselves as a threat. This way, if he turned out to be an enemy, they could destroy him without destroying his ship.

Of course, their strategy assumed that he was more dangerous behind the firing controls of a laser cannon than he was on the ground.

It was a poor assumption.

The Yavin 4 hangar deck was a hub of bustling activity. X-wing fighters set off for missions while others limped onto the tarmac, bruised and battered. Maintenance droids and deck officers raced from ship to ship, scavenging parts from one to fix another, refitting and refueling with efficient haste. X-7 could see with a glance that there were fewer ships than needed, fewer parts, fewer pilots, fewer everything.

It was nearly laughable, the idea that an operation like this could stand up to the Empire. Some might have called it brave. X-7 knew better.

"Careful with that, friend," he told the Rebel guard, nodding at the blaster. "I'd hate for you to accidentally blow a hole through me." He kept his tone casual.

"Wouldn't be anything accidental about it," the guard growled. "Now how about you tell me where you got that landing code."

"From Lieutenant Jez Planchet," X-7 said. "He recruited me about six months ago. Gave me orders to bring you a message — and then report for duty. I'm ready to serve the Rebel Alliance, wherever I'm needed." He was prepared for this. He was prepared for anything.

The guard narrowed his eyes and flicked a finger across his datapad. "So you ran into Planchet on Kashyyyk, eh?"

X-7 forced a thin smile. "Lieutenant Planchet's been deep undercover on Malastare for the last year. *Sir.*" How amusing that they thought they could trick him. It was like playing a game with a child — carefully manipulating the playing field to give him the illusion that he was among equals.

The guard gave a terse nod. "And you have some kind of proof that you are who you say you are?"

"Actually, I *haven't* said who I am, yet," X-7 pointed out. Any respect he might have had was quickly fading. This was no way to run an interrogation. They hadn't even confiscated his weapons: He could kill half the men in this hangar without breaking a sweat. "S'ree Bonard. Pleased to meet you." He held out a datapad. "Here are my ID docs, and the data Planchet had me smuggle out. They're plans for some kind of new Imperial ship. Lieutenant Planchet wanted them to go straight to Dodonna."

In fact, all Lieutenant Planchet had wanted was a release from the torture he'd indured in his Imperial prison cell. He had indeed spent several months undercover on Malastare, completely cut off from his Rebel allies.

Which meant when the Empire arrived at his door, he had no one to call for help.

And when the Empire's expert interrogators began their work, he had no hope of rescue.

According to the Commander, Planchet had stayed silent at first — but the human body could only tolerate so much pain. In the end, he had yielded all his Rebel secrets, begging only for an end to the torture.

And he was given what he'd asked for.

Dead men felt no pain.

The Rebel perused the datapad carefully. X-7 knew what he would find. Impeccable credentials proving he was S'ree Bonard, a man who'd never existed. Falsified blueprints for a battleship that would never be built. A certifying thumbprint and Alliance codes from Lieutenant Planchet, whose rebellion had ended with a whimper and a bolt of blasterfire. Out-of-date codes, yes — but what more could one expect from a man who'd been undercover for nearly a year?

"This all appears in order," the guard said, the suspicion fading from his voice. "I better get this info to General Dodonna."

"Lieutenant Planchet specifically requested that I deliver the blueprints personally," X-7 said.

The Rebel shook his head. "Not gonna happen. We've got some new security protocols — can't have you leaving the hangar until everything's been checked out."

X-7 feigned disappointment. No need to reveal that the hangar was exactly where he wanted to be. "I've been in that ship for a long time," he complained. "I was really looking forward to a good meal, a hot shower —"

"Trust me, I've been there, pal," the guard cut in. "But we all got to do our part for the Rebellion. And right now, your part is to stay right here until I get you clearance. Understood?"

X-7 nodded. "Understood."

The guard left, promising to return with official clearance within the hour. And X-7 was left to his own devices. Forbidden from leaving the hangar.

Which, of course, was the last thing he wanted to do.

He sauntered up to a scarred, rusted Corellian cruiser that matched the specs of a ship Leia Organa had been known to use. A team of maintenance droids was working on the starboard dorsal engine while a slim, brown-haired man in a deck officer's uniform struggled with the dorsal rectenna dish.

When he paused, looking around for one of his tools, X-7 tossed him a fusioncutter.

"Trouble with the sensor array?" he asked.

"Trouble with everything," the deck officer grumbled. "Can't believe the piece of junk even flies."

"Maybe it doesn't," X-7 said agreeably. "Ever think about grounding her?"

"Ground the *Falcon*?" The deck officer spliced together a set of wires on the electro photo receptor. "Don't let Solo hear you say that."

"Oh?" *Solo.* X-7 filed the name away, and waited. He preferred not to ask questions. It was more effective to stay quiet and let your target fill the silence.

"I shouldn't even be working on her," the deck officer grumbled. "Solo never lets anyone near her but that Wookiee. Fine with me, I say. But they're off in some *briefing*, just talking, talking, talking, while I'm the one who has to actually *do* something, is all I'm saying. So I'm stuck mucking about in the grease. Like I don't have better things to do than more repairs on a ship that belongs on the junk heap."

"Think you'll get it done by the time they have to leave?" X-7 kept his voice casual. Unconcerned.

"I got a few more hours, and only a couple more repairs to make. Shouldn't be a problem."

"In that case, maybe you've got time to take a look at something for me?" X-7 said, a new plan beginning to coalesce. "Shouldn't take more than a second — I could really use an expert opinion."

The deck officer grinned. "That's all I got, buddy. Besides, be nice to work with someone who actually appreciated me, is all I'm saying. That Wookiee's always grunting and growling every time I get my wrench near his deflector shield. And last time I was dumb enough try to touch the hyperdrive? Well, lucky I still have both my arms, is all I'm saying."

"It's right over here," X-7 said, leading the deck officer into a secluded corner of the spaceport. A large pile of damaged generators shielded them from view. "I've been having quite a problem."

The deck officer looked confused when X-7 stopped. Except for a few crates of spare parts, the area was empty. "There's no ship here — hey!" His shout faded as the injected nerve toxin took effect. The man was dead before he hit the ground.

X-7 stripped him of his uniform, then slid his body into a crevice in the generator pile where, with any luck, it wouldn't be discovered for days. "Problem solved."

It took only a few minutes to slip aboard the *Millennium Falcon* and access the navigational computer, which had been programmed on a course for Muunilinst. Now he knew where they were headed — and, after making a few modifications to the ship's systems, he knew exactly how he would intercept them.

After that, he needed only to find himself a way off

the moon. And what could be simpler? He had the Preybird. He had his blaster.

And moments later, he had a young, terrified Rebel pilot willing to do anything he asked. A blaster muzzle digging into the ribcage tended to have that effect on people. A more experienced soldier might have turned the situation to his advantage, realizing that X-7 couldn't afford to shoot. Not if he wanted to get out alive. A more experienced soldier certainly would have known better than to climb into the Preybird as ordered, and relay the series of codes necessary to gain departure clearance.

A more experienced soldier likely would not have believed X-7's promise. "Do as I say, and I'll let you live."

But X-7 had chosen well, and this soldier was no soldier at all. He was little more than a scared boy, wearing his uniform like a costume.

And, once he'd served his purpose, he was disposable.

There was no need to use the blaster. The vacuum of space did the job just fine, without leaving behind a bloody mess. As the pilot's body drifted away into the black, X-7 set a course for Muunilinst. It was time to put his plan in motion.

*　　*　　*

The man he needed proved easy to track down. Soon his pinched, grizzled face was looming on the communicator screen.

"It'll cost you," the pilot said, once he heard X-7's proposal.

"Name your price," X-7 suggested. "My employer has rather deep pockets."

"And you're sure it's safe? Solo's got a reputation, you know. You'd have to be crazy to go up against the *Millennium Falcon*. Especially in a TIE fighter. Those things practically explode if you sneeze on them."

"I've taken care of the *Falcon*. Just show up at the coordinates I've given you. It's completely safe." X-7 smiled, offering up a perfect simulation of candid sincerity. "You have my personal guarantee."

The Muunilinst system was still hours away when X-7 began his transformation. He began with the physical — X-7 had been taught to believe that change happened from the outside in. And his specialized medpac made change easy.

Painful, but easy.

Ignoring the localized nerve anesthetic, he used a small durasteel mallet to crush his nasal bones. He set them with the bone fuser, adding a bump and a slight curve that gave his face a completely different look. Colored lenses turned his eyes a bright green, and a black tattoo across his neck marked him as a member of the A'mari. This was the former ruling class of Malano III, the planet he would claim as his own.

The chances of Leia knowing anything about Malano III or the A'mari were low, but X-7 left nothing to chance.

His new identity was that of a warrior, and a warrior needed scars. He raked the sonic scalpel in a jagged line from his left eye to his chin, pleasuring in the pain.

There were easier ways, but he preferred the pain. It kept his mind clear. Reminded him of the stakes.

Reminded him of the Commander, and the only home he'd ever known.

A blaster set on stun, aimed at the chest, the back, the shoulders.

A simple applicaton of bacta, and his false identity was complete: a battle-scarred warrior, fresh from the front lines.

X-7 called up the details of his new persona on the datapad, running his eyes over and over them, although they were already stored in his head.

"Tobin Elad," he repeated aloud, testing the new name on his tongue.

"I am Tobin Elad." He watched himself saying it in a plane of mirrored transparisteel, mastering every twitch of the eye, every quirk of the lips, any and every sign that might give away the lie.

He practiced smiling, lighting his dead eyes with a life that almost seemed real.

He practiced laughing.

He practiced the lie of his humanity until he nearly believed it himself. And then he knew he was ready. X-7 would sink beneath the surface, poised, waiting for Tobin Elad to get the job done. And when he did, X-7 would emerge. And strike.

He wiped the details of his false identity from the datapad and called up the picure of Leia, the one he'd first seen. It was a few years old, from a time before her eyes had taken on their sad, haunted look. She was smiling, her long hair wrapped around her head in an elaborate braid. Her head was inclined slightly forward, as if she were about to share a secret with the holocam.

This was the Leia he planned to target. This Leia still existed, he was sure of it. The younger, sweeter Leia who lived beneath the cynical Rebel. The one who longed to connect with someone who could truly understand her, with whom she could share all her secrets.

"Your wait is almost over, princess," X-7 whispered, his eyes fixed on her face. "I'm on my way."

'm bringing us out of hyperdrive now," Han informed his passengers. "We'll be just outside the Muunilinst system, so it should be smooth sailing from here on in."

"It's about time," Leia complained. "If I have to be stuck in this tin can with you for any longer, I'll scream."

Stuck with me? Han thought in frustration. *She* was the one who'd been pestering him the whole trip — *check this, try this, have you thought of that,* and on and on. The princess just didn't know how to keep her mouth shut.

"Feel free to get out here," Han retorted, gesturing to the gleaming strands of stars whipping past the ship. "Say the word and I'll just drop you right out the hatch."

"You'd really do it, wouldn't you?" Leia asked incredulously.

"You bet I would, sweetheart."

Chewbacca growled.

"Oh yes I *would*," Han insisted. "And if you don't stop taking her side, you can go with her, you hairy fuzzball."

Chewbacca yowled.

Han rolled his eyes as he took the ship out of hyperdrive. "Since when are you so sensitive, Chewie? I was just — whoa!" The ship shuddered.

"What's happening?" Leia cried, almost tumbling into his lap. She caught herself just in time.

"Someone's shooting at us, princess. In case you hadn't noticed." Han pulled the *Falcon* around, trying to get a glimpse of his attacker. The guy was right on his tail.

Han jerked the ship up, then hard to starboard, dodging another blast of laserfire.

"There's someone shooting at us!" Luke cried, already scrambling down the tube that led to the ventral quad laser cannons.

"You don't say." Han accelerated, trying to get some distance from the attacker — who was a good shot. He took the *Falcon* into a screaming dive, then pulled up, *hard*, drawing level with the enemy. "Gotcha!" he shouted, as the TIE fighter came into view. "Kid, why aren't we blowing this Imperial slugbrain out of the sky?"

"Something's wrong!" Even over the staticky com-link, the alarm in Luke's voice came through loud and clear. "The weapons system is offline."

"Well, get it *on*line!" Han jerked his head at Chewie, but the Wookiee was already on his way, closely followed by R2-D2.

"Sir, might I suggest evasive action?" C-3PO put in.

"Excellent suggestion," Han said through gritted teeth. He took them into a corkscrew dive. "Wish I'd thought of that myself."

"Still, we *must* get the lasers back online, Captain Solo," C-3PO added. The bucket of bolts was just a fount of helpful advice. "Otherwise I'm afraid I esti-mate our odds at seven thousand, three hundred thirty six to —"

"What did I say about quoting me odds?" Han increased the forward thrust. The ship bucked and shuddered as Imperial laserfire blasted their deflector shield. They were too close to the moons of Muunilinst to safely go into hyperdrive, but if he could get just a lit-tle room —

"What are you doing?" Leia asked in alarm.

"Running away," Han snapped. "Unless you still think that's the coward's way."

"No, running away is good," Leia said quickly. "Let's go. But why can't we just go into hyper —" Leia fell silent as a second ship dropped out of hyperdrive.

"Company," Han said grimly. A rusted Preybird starfighter. No match for the *Falcon* — if the *Falcon* could shoot. He had to get out of there, fast. Their shields couldn't take another direct hit. And if the deflector system failed, too . . .

"Wait!" Leia gripped his shoulder. "Look!"

The new ship swooped toward the TIE. Laserfire lit up the sky. The fighter swung sharply to port, returning fire. It scored a direct hit on the Preybird.

"What's he doing?" Han said, wondering what kind of nut was piloting the ship. "That old ship can't take that kind of fire."

The Preybird dodged the next round and unleashed a laser blast of its own. The ships danced around each other, laserfire exploding on all sides. Han could do nothing but watch.

He hated it.

"What's going on with those laser cannons?" he shouted. This was *his* fight.

"No luck," Luke called back. "The cannons are jammed and even if we could get them working, we have no targeting capability. The whole system's gone haywire!"

"Great," Han muttered. "Just great."

He swung the ship around and accelerated, heading straight for the TIE fighter.

"What are you doing?" Leia asked, panic filling her voice. "What happened to running *away*?"

"Change of plans," Han said, pushing the ship faster.

"We don't have any weapons!"

"Glad you've been paying attention." The TIE loomed in his sights. "But *he* doesn't know that."

"That other ship is doing just fine —"

"I don't know about you, Highness, but I fight my own battles."

"And how, exactly, are we supposed to fight without any weapons?"

The TIE fighter loomed in the viewscreen. They were almost on top of it. "We'll figure that out when we —"

"He's retreating!" Leia exclaimed.

"Of course he is," Han said calmly, trying to disguise his shock. And relief.

The Preybird took off after the fleeing TIE Fighter, firing a single shot to its starboard solar array wing. The Imperial ship exploded.

Han tensed, waiting for the Preybird to make a move. Sure, the other pilot had helped them out of a jam. But in his experience, people only helped you when they wanted something. Maybe this guy wanted his cargo. Or his ship.

"How we doing with those laser cannons?" Han asked nervously.

A transmission came in over the comlink.

"Corellian freighter, this is . . . request assistance . . ." Only a few clear words bubbled up through the storm of static. "Damaged my . . . and power generator . . . forced to . . . not sure if I . . . please send —"

The call cut off abruptly. They watched in horror as the ship belched out a plume of black exhaust, then dipped precariously toward a nearby moon. The Preybird glowed orange with heat as it plummeted through the atmosphere — and then disappeared beneath the clouds.

Leia's eyes widened with horror. "We have to go after him!"

"I thought the only thing that mattered was the *mission*, princess," Han teased, quoting words she'd fired at him a hundred times.

She looked at him in disgust. "He *saved* us. Now he's our responsibility."

"Hey, no one asked for his help," Han grumbled. But he'd already set a course for the surface. That was the thing about Leia. She never understood when he was joking. It was almost like she *wanted* to think the worst of him.

So let her, he thought. Why should he care?

He shouldn't.

But he did.

It took them almost an hour to find the crash site. Magnetic disturbances in the moon's atmosphere made it difficult to pick up the Preybird's distress beacon until they were right on top of it. But they finally found the ship, or what was left of it. The Preybird lay at the base of a jagged cliffside, smashed nearly to pieces.

Leia caught her breath. "Do you think he's . . . ?"

"Well, I doubt he's having a tea party in there," Han said, keeping his voice light to cover his concern. No reason to upset the others — at least until there was a reason. "But only one way to find out."

The moon was uninhabited, and Han could see why. The air was dense and murky, rich with the scent of oxite. The bluish globe of Muunilinst hung overhead, on the opposite side of the sky from the dim, jaundiced sun. Scrub brush littered the dusty ground, spotting the dirt-gray hills of rock and clay that stretched to the horizon. There was no movement or sound in the heavy air; the world seemed still and dead.

Except.

"There's no one inside," Luke reported, after examining the Preybird wreckage. Black scorch marks scraped across what was left of the hull. "At least we know he's not dead."

"Not yet." Han pointed toward the large, inhuman

65

tracks leading toward and then away from the ship, disappearing into the hills.

A thin groove in the dirt followed the footsteps, as if the creature had dragged something behind it.

The groove was stained with a trail of blood.

lood seeped through the bandage. A crimson stain spread swiftly across his shirt. He'd slashed himself deeper than intended, and could feel the life pumping out of him with each step.

No matter.

They would find him when he was ready to be found. And when that happened, a graver injury could only work in his favor.

No one would ever guess that the gashes had come from his fire blade rather than the crash.

X-7 had waited an hour before activating the distress beacon — and in the meantime, he'd been busy. After laying the trail, he'd doubled back, lying in wait for his "rescuers" to arrive. Now he shadowed them as they followed the tracks he'd laid, leaving the Wookiee and the little R2 droid to guard the ship. He watched closely as the princess forged ahead, the two men scrambling to keep up with her.

So the princess was foolhardy, her friends powerless to stop her from blundering into trouble.

Interesting.

X-7 filed it away for future reference. He tread silently and stayed close. From a few paces behind, he could hear them bickering, could hear the protocol droid complaining, could hear the two men dither over which way to go as the tracks faded.

They didn't look like much of a threat.

Still, X-7 knew better than to trust his first impression. Many men had made that mistake when encountering him. Few lived to make it a second time.

Wincing at the pain in his shoulder, he drew out his dart shooter. Took aim at the taller male, and fired.

The man slapped at the back of his neck, then examined his palm, likely looking for the insect that had bitten him. Then shrugged, and continued walking.

X-7 paused, letting them get further ahead.

He didn't want to be too close when the pheromone dart did its job, releasing a scent that would draw the nearest reek. When the beast found a group of humans instead of a potential mate, X-7 suspected it would be rather . . . displeased.

Once the creature attacked, X-7 would draw closer

again, watching them defend themselves. It would be the best way to gauge their weaknesses. And, if the beast was able to slaughter the one exuding the pheromones, so much the better. X-7 would intercede before it could harm the princess.

She could hardly refuse to trust him after that.

There was a faint roar in the distance. A moment later, the ground began to shake.

Here it comes, X-7 thought. *Let the games begin.*

Luke grabbed hold of the nearest boulder, trying to keep his balance as the ground rumbled. "Moonquake?" he asked.

Leia shook her head, pointing a finger over his shoulder. Luke whirled around. A giant beast lumbered toward them on legs thick as tree trunks. Its hunched back rose to nearly three times Luke's height. A horn stuck out of each side of its face, while a third spurted from its forehead, sharp as a knife and thicker at its base than a human torso.

"It looks like a reek." Luke drew his lightsaber. The Hutts on his home planet sometimes used them as execution animals. "They're mostly herbivores, but . . ."

"*But?*" Han yelped, lunging out of the way as the reek swiped at him with a trunklike leg.

"But when their skin turns all reddish brown like that, it usually means they've got a taste for meat," Luke admitted.

Han whipped out his blaster and took aim, but the blasterfire bounced off the reek's tough hide. "I'm no one's meat!" he shouted, scrambling up a shallow hill of rocks to get a better angle. The reek lowered its head and charged.

"Get down, princess!" Han called to Leia as he dove out of the way just in time. She ducked behind the nearest rocky outcropping. C-3PO was already cowering beneath it. Leia elbowed him aside and began blasting at the reek with her laser pistol.

Han fired again, but the reek only grunted, charging straight through the blaster bolts.

Luke raised his lightsaber, but froze. What good was a lightsaber against a creature like this? Even if he could get close enough to strike, he'd probably be crushed before he could do any good.

A lightsaber is the only weapon a Jedi needs, Ben had told him.

Easy for Ben to say, Luke thought now. *He knew how to use it.*

"Forget the toy!" Han yelled, running at full speed from the lumbering reek. He paused every few seconds to turn back and shoot, aiming for a different spot each time, in hopes of finding a weakness in the thick hide. But it was no use, and the reek showed no signs of tiring. "Blast the thing before it has me for dinner!"

"The blasters aren't hurting it!" Luke shouted back. At the sound of his voice, the reek turned around, as if noticing him for the first time. It grunted, stomped, and then took off for Luke. It was too close, and coming too fast. He couldn't get out of the way.

Luke fumbled for his blaster, but it got caught in its holster. The reek drew closer.

"Hey, what about me?" Han yelled, trying to distract it again. "Dinner's this way, you horn-faced jerk!"

But the reek was fixed on Luke.

He knew if he tried to run, he could be trampled beneath the beast's mammoth feet before he got more than a few paces. So he held his ground. He raised his lightsaber, focusing on the shimmering blue blade, trying to block out his fear.

Luke remembered Han's strategy with the TIE fighter. *I may not be strong enough to kill the reek*, Luke thought, *but the reek doesn't know that*.

He ran *toward* the beast.

"Luke!" Leia screamed. "No!"

Luke stumbled over a large rock bulging out of the dirt. He hurtled wildly through the air, blade outstretched, and landed with a thump a few feet away, flat on his face. A keening howl split his eardrums, and then, with a thunderous crack, the world seemed to crumble beneath him.

A moment later, all was silent and still.

Luke rolled over and looked up at the concerned faces of his friends. "I'm not dead," he said in confusion.

Han laughed, but Luke could see the concern beneath the smile. "Don't sound so disappointed, kid."

Luke sat up, his head throbbing. "What happened?"

"You tripped and fell flat on your face," Han said.

"Yeah, that part I remember." He rubbed the back of his head, then twisted it from side to side, freezing as he caught sight of the mighty reek, *dead*.

"Oh. Right," Han said, following his gaze. "There was also the part where your lightsaber sliced our friend here wide open. Poor guy was just trying to get a snack."

"That 'poor guy' nearly had us all for a three-course meal!" Leia exclaimed, giving Han a light smack on the shoulder. She tugged Luke up off the ground. "Are you sure you're okay?"

Luke couldn't take his eyes off the reek. He'd really done it, he'd saved the day — with his *lightsaber*.

If only he hadn't done it by accident.

"Master Luke, I think I've picked up the trail again," C-3PO reported, gesturing to the bloody footsteps that tramped further into the hills. Luke shuddered. Now that he knew what kind of creature was responsible for those tracks, he was even more worried about the fate of the injured pilot. They had to find him before it was too late.

For almost half an hour, they followed the trail across the rocky landscape. It ended at the mouth of a cave. Han and Luke exchanged a glance. Luke guessed they were both thinking the same thing: *something* had gone into that cave. Probably something they didn't want to meet. Leia gave them both a disgusted look, then strode inside.

"After you," Han said dryly. But he hurried after her. Luke followed.

"If it's all the same to you, I'll just wait out here, Master Luke," C-3PO called. "I think I can be of the most service if I . . ." His voice faded away as they penetrated deeper into the dark cave.

"I think I see something," Leia whispered, striding ahead.

"Yeah, but does it see *us*?" Han muttered.

There was a body sprawled against the far wall of the cave. Leia hurried over, kneeling by its side. Luke and Han approached more slowly, keeping an eye on the mouth of the cave.

The man was bloodied and pale, but his eyes were open. "You shouldn't have followed me," he rasped, struggling to breathe. "It's coming b —" He broke off into a fit of coughing. "This is where it li —" He exploded into more coughs, then fell backward, exhausted by the effort.

"What's he trying to say?" Han asked.

Sensing a familiar rumble beneath his feet, Luke drew his lightsaber. "I think he's saying, *This is where it lives!*" he cried, as a reek burst into the cave. Leia flung herself across the wounded pilot, shielding him with her body. Han grabbed his blaster.

The reek lowered its horn and charged.

"Blasting it doesn't work!" Luke complained. "Let me handle this."

"You had so much fun the first time?" Han shot back. "That was just a fluke. Keep out of the way and try not to get yourself hurt."

"But if you shoot that off in here, you'll —" Before Luke could finish, Han pulled the trigger, aiming for the mouth of the cave. Blaster fire ricocheted off the roof, dislodging a hail of giant rocks that rained down on the reek's head. The beast went down in a heap.

"See, kid?" Han said triumphantly. "I told you I'd . . ."

He broke off as the ceiling continued to crumble, an avalanche of rocks tumbling down. They pressed themselves against the cave wall as clouds of dust billowed up from the massive collapse.

Moments later, the thunder of falling rocks died away. The dust cleared. And a wall of solid rock blocked off their only escape.

". . . handle it," Han finished in a weak voice.

They were trapped.

CHAPTER NINE

"Don't you look at me like that," Han warned the others, as they turned to glare at him. "It's not my fault!"

"Oh, really?" Leia said dryly.

"Look, princess, I don't know what it's like where you come from, but where *I* come from, you *shoot* the giant scaly monster that's trying to eat you." As he spoke, Han ran his hands along the wall of rock, searching an opening. If he could just pry a few of the rocks loose, he might be able to dig them out.

But hard as he tugged, none of the rocks would budge. They were wedged solid.

"I didn't have a choice," Han insisted, aware that he was getting dangerously close to whining. "What did you want me to do?"

"You could have let *Luke* handle it, like he asked," Leia pointed out.

"The kid and his glorified nerf-steak knife?" Han gaped at Leia. Was she *crazy*? "We'd all be reek feed by now!" He paused, glancing at Luke, who was standing off to the edge of the cave, his back to the rest of them. Probably practicing some kind of Jedi meditation trick. Luke always picked the strangest times to go all mystical on them. "No offense."

"Offense taken," Luke murmured, concentrating on whatever foolish thing he was doing.

Han turned back to the princess, who was still tending to the wounded pilot. If she would just let him *explain* what he'd been thinking . . .

You weren't quite *thinking, buddy*, said an annoying voice in his head. *That's the problem*. He ignored it.

"Look, C-3PO's out there," Han said. "Maybe he'll be able to dig us out."

Leia didn't have to say anything, she just looked at him. Han sighed. "Fine. Then I'm sure he'll go get Chewie. A Wookiee is just what we need." The comlinks weren't working, thanks to all the magnetic interference, but surely the droid would figure out what to do on his own. "He's probably on his way back to the ship right now . . . unless he stopped to impress a reek with one of his six million languages," Han added under his breath. "Or fell in a ditch."

Leia glared. "If we die in here, I'll kill you."

Han opened his mouth to point out that didn't make any sense . . . but stopped himself just in time. "We're not going to die, Your Highness," he assured her. "I'm sure even you can get by for a few hours without your ladies-in-waiting, or whatever it is you princesses need to survive."

"Maybe *I* can," she snapped, "but *he* can't." She nodded toward the injured man, lying in a pool of blood. "I've done what I can for him here, but the wound is bleeding out of control. We have to get him back to the ship. A few hours might be too long."

The pilot groaned. "That's some bedside manner you have there," he said.

Han arched an eyebrow at Leia. She scowled. "I thought he was unconscious!" she said, defensively.

"You're quite the medical expert," Han teased.

"I'd suggest *you* take over," Leia shot back, "but you'd probably try to *blast* him back to health."

"Hey!" Han protested. But Leia turned her back to him, murmuring something comforting to the pilot.

"Some rescue attempt," the man complained, his voice weak.

"Try a little gratitude," Han suggested. If he was strong enough to dish it out, he was strong enough to take it. "We're the ones doing *you* a favor."

"A favor might have been letting me rescue myself," the man said.

Han snorted. "Yeah, you were doing a great job, lying here on the floor of the cave waiting to get eaten. *Brilliant* plan."

"Reeks are herbivores," the pilot said, in a superior tone.

Han *hated* superior tones. "Funny, I guess no one told that guy," he said, gesturing toward the definitely carnivorous reek lying dead on the floor of the cave. "Face it, buddy, if it weren't for me, you'd be lunch."

"You're right." His voice broke off into another coughing fit. "*This* is a definite improvement."

"Han, leave the poor man alone," Leia said angrily. "He needs his rest."

"Me?" Han asked, incredulous. "*He* started it."

Leia shook her head. "I know you have the *mind* of a five year old, but that's no reason to act like one."

"You — ! How can you — ? I — !" Han sputtered, searching for the perfect response.

Finally, he told himself it wasn't worth it. He turned to Luke, who was fumbling with his lightsaber over on the far end of the cave. "How about you? Don't you want to tell me what I'm doing wrong?"

Luke offered up a serene smile. "Actually, I was thinking I might get us out of here . . . unless you two aren't done arguing yet?"

Leia looked up, surprised. "You can get us out of here?"

"He's bluffing," Han said confidently. Then he took a closer look at Luke. "You're bluffing, right?"

Ignoring him, Luke strode toward the wall of rock blocking their exit, and plunged his glowing lightsaber into the pile. It sliced through the rocks like they were made of air. "I tested it first," Luke explained, "to make sure the beam was strong enough — and to make sure it wouldn't just cause the rocks to cave in even more."

"Thinking before you act," Leia said, giving Han a pointed look. "Imagine that."

Luke began cutting through the rock, methodically working the saber back and forth to carve out an opening. It was slow going, and Han could see it was going to take a while — but it would work.

"Good thinking," he said. Luke was a little clueless some of the time — okay, most of the time. But Han had to admit it: The kid came through in a pinch.

"I *told* you the lightsaber was a valuable weapon," Luke said.

"Hey, don't get ahead of yourself," Han argued. "Slicing and dicing a pile of rocks doesn't exactly qualify something as a *weapon*. It's no blaster."

"Lucky for us," Luke pointed out.

Han grimaced. "If you're going to keep throwing that back in my face every time I —"

"Not to interrupt," the pilot interrupted, "but less

arguing and more cutting would probably be —" He broke off abruptly.

"Probably be what?" Han asked irritably. What made this guy think he could tell them what to do?

"He's out cold," Leia said, concern filling her voice. "Luke, you've got to hurry! We have to get him back to the ship *soon* or . . ."

She didn't finish, but she didn't have to.

Han joined Luke's side, pushing rocks out of the way as Luke's glowing blade widened the opening. He'd seen men lose that much blood before, and he knew what it meant. That pilot had to return to the ship soon — or he wouldn't be going anywhere at all, ever again.

Leia rested a hand gently on the pilot's forehead. He was still so pale, but at least the fire no longer burned beneath his skin. They had brought him back to the ship and soaked his wounds in bacta, but beyond that there was little they could do for him. The *Millennium Falcon* was equipped with only the most basic medical provisions.

As Han, Luke, and Chewbacca worked to put the weapons systems back online, Leia had sat by the anonymous pilot's bed, waiting for him to wake up. It had been nearly a day.

We don't even know who he is, Leia thought, watching his eyeballs twitch faintly beneath his lids. *If he dies out here, no one who loves him will ever know what happened.*

She tried not to think about it. After all, his pulse was strong. His wounds were healing. There was no reason to think he wouldn't make a full recovery.

If he ever woke up.

They owed him so much, she thought. He'd saved them from certain death at the hands of the Empire. Whoever he was, whatever his motives, there was no escaping that truth. They owed him.

"But if you want us to pay you back, you're going to have to wake up," she murmured.

"You drive a hard bargain."

Leia started in surprise, jerking her hand away from his forehead. "You're awake!"

"Seems that way." He smiled, and tried to sit up, groaning at the effort.

Gently, she pushed him back down to the bunk. They were in a cramped room just off the main hold, where Han had stored his meager medical supplies. "Easy," she told him. "You lost a lot of blood."

He grimaced. "That wasn't part of the plan."

"What plan?"

A strange, blank look flashed across his face, and then it was gone, so quickly that Leia thought she might have imagined it. Especially when he smiled. His eyes sparkled with good humor, and some of the color seemed to come back into his face. "The plan where I rescue the fair maiden and reap her eternal gratitude."

Leia suppressed a grin. This was still a stranger, she reminded herself, and they were at war. You couldn't trust every would-be hero with a charming smile. *Just look at Han*, she thought. Hero one moment, scoundrel the next.

The galaxy could be a confusing place.

"If you're well enough to flirt, you're well enough to answer some questions," she said sternly. "Want to tell me what you were doing out there, fighting someone else's battle?"

"Is that your way of saying thank you?" the pilot asked. "Because if so, you and your blast-happy friend have some work to do on the etiquette front."

Leia sighed. "*Thank you*. Now . . . what were you doing out there?"

"What were *you* doing out there?" he countered. "Who are you people, anyway?"

"I asked first," Leia said, biting down hard on the corners of her lips to trap another grin.

"Indeed you did." The pilot looked thoughtful for a moment. "Truth?"

"That would be nice."

He raised a hand, wincing at the effort. She shook, being careful not to squeeze too hard. "Tobin Elad," he told her. "Dissident, guerilla warrior, exile, orphan, and rather atrocious poet. Though not in that order."

"Leia," she said, keeping her surname to herself.

"Professional damsel in distress?" he suggested,

when it was clear she wouldn't be offering any additional information.

"I prefer to rescue *myself*, thank you very much."

"I'll keep that in mind for the future," he said lightly. "Wouldn't want to overstep."

"You call yourself a warrior," Leia said. "That means you have an enemy."

He grew serious at once. "We all have an enemy. The Empire." Again, he tried to push himself into a sitting position. This time, despite the pain, he made it upright. "Though I suppose some of us have more reason to fight than others."

Leia suspected that the pain written across his face had nothing to do with his wounded shoulder. "And your reason?" she asked softly.

"*Reasons*," he admitted. "Three of them. Or hundreds of thousands. Depending on how you count." He fell silent.

Leia waited, letting him go forward at his own pace.

He kept his eyes fixed over her shoulder, gazing intently at the wall of instrument panels behind her head. She took in the faded bruises on his arms and torso, the network of scars criss-crossing his weathered face. He was a few years younger than Han, but the darkness in his eyes made him appear much, much older.

"At first, I wanted only peace," he said, his voice barely audible. "Peaceful coexistence with the Empire. Preservation of our way of life. Have you ever been to Malano III?"

Leia shook her head. She knew it was a world just beyond the galactic core, but she had never been.

"It's a beautiful place," he said. "Trees everywhere. Even our cities were idylls of green, laced through with crystalline blue rivers. And we are a peaceful people." He frowned. "*Were*. We *were* peaceful. But that wasn't enough for the Empire. No, it wasn't enough that we obey quietly. They wanted our cities, they wanted our *land*. They wanted to turn our quiet planet into a home for their armies and their weapons installations. Cover the land with barracks and factories. Turn its citizens into workers. 'Work,' that was their term." His face twisted. "I called it what it was. Slavery."

"The Empire must have appreciated that," Leia said wryly.

"Not so much," he agreed. "Those of us who objected were soon driven out. We who had been peaceful objectors became saboteurs, sneaking into the city in the dead of night, setting explosives, struggling to regain control." He shook his head. "We were fools. I see that now. Insane to think the Empire could be deterred."

"It's never foolish to fight for what's right," Leia said fiercely.

"It's foolish to deny what you know to be the truth. And the truth is, we were few, we were weak. The Empire was strong. If they'd only punished us . . ." His throat choked off the words. Then he cleared his throat. When he spoke again, his tone was nearly expressionless. "Mirabel, that was our capital. They used thermal detonators to create a firestorm that consumed the whole city. Thousands upon thousands died. Everyone I'd ever cared about. Everyone I'd ever known. My wife . . ." He hung his head, and continued in a whisper. "My child."

"I'm sorry." They were such small, pathetic words. Nothing, in the face of what he'd lost.

And Leia understood loss.

"It was a long time ago," Elad said, his voice stony. Leia recognized that tone, that hardness. You had to block out the storm of emotions — forget the past — if you were going to go on. "I'm on my own now, hitting back at the Empire where and when I can. That's what I was doing when we crossed paths — I figured if I could get my hands on a TIE fighter, I could fly right into the heart of the Empire, really do some damage before they caught on."

"A single ship against the Imperial Fleet?" Leia asked in horror. "But that's —"

Certain death.

He nodded. "I guess I owe you and your crew an apology. I'd been planning to force that Imperial into a crash landing on the moon — but I guess I chased him right into your path."

"So saving us ruined your plan?"

"Revenge can wait a little longer," Elad said. "To be honest, it's the only thing left keeping me going. When you've lost as much as I have . . ." He shook his head. "You wouldn't understand. I hope you'll never have to."

Leia rested a hand lightly on his. "I understand."

She needed only to say the word, and he would see.

Alderaan.

It filled her mind, every day, every minute. Their faces, their voices. The lush, green parks, filled with children on a summer's day. The sweet scent of t'iil, blossoming over a meadow. Her father's embrace.

Gone.

They lived inside of her, but she trapped them within. The pain was too fresh, too raw. It was too hard.

And yet suddenly, it seemed all too easy to let it out.

"Sometimes I fear the fight is all that keeps me going," she told him. "I draw breath, I eat, I move forward, only because I know the fight must continue. Maybe that's why I fight so hard. Because if I didn't have that —" Leia stopped. She'd never admitted that to anyone before. Maybe not even to herself.

And this was a *stranger*. What was she doing?

"If you didn't have that, you fear there'd be nothing left?" It didn't sound like a question.

Leia stood up abruptly. "I should let the others know you're awake," she said brusquely. "They've been concerned."

"I'm not going anywhere," Elad pointed out. "They can wait."

She was tempted to stay, to talk — and that decided her. "Someone will be back to check on you soon," she told him, backing out of the small room. She needed to get away from this man — to stay away from him. He tempted her to trust too much, too easily, and that way led only to danger. "Lie back. Rest."

He followed orders, poorly disguising a sigh of relief as his head hit the pillow. "Thank you, Leia. For sitting with me. It seems I haven't had anyone to talk to — really *talk* to — in a long time. It felt surprisingly good."

"Sometimes you just need someone to listen to you," Leia said, shifting uncomfortably under the weight of his stare.

"Yes," he said, gazing so intently that she feared he could see right into her head. "Sometimes you do."

The severity of his injury had been unexpected, but it had worked to his advantage.

X-7 made everything work to his advantage; it was the only way he'd stayed alive for as long as he had.

The princess had bought the act completely, he could

tell from the glassy sheen that fell across her eyes when he unspooled the lies about a dead wife and child. Soon she would open up to him, tell him whatever he needed to know.

X-7 regained his strength quickly, but feigned weakness over the course of the next two days. Hobbling around the ship gave him a chance to observe the crew. And certainly no one would expect the brave, wounded hero to pose a threat.

They'd put the weapons systems back online, and were now in a stable orbit around Muunilinst. X-7 suspected they were waiting to decide what to do with him before they made their next move. His next job was to convince them he could be trusted with the content of their Rebel mission — the first of many Rebel secrets he would possess.

He bided his time; he watched. Humans were sad creatures, he thought, so unaware of their own selves, their own weaknesses. Leia and the captain, Han, for example. They argued ceaselessly, oblivious of the energy that lay beneath the surface of their every encounter. Neither understood the unspoken bond they shared. But X-7 saw it, and this was knowledge he could exploit.

And the boy . . . now, there was an interesting case. When Luke had faced the reek with his lightsaber, X-7 had nearly given himself away with a gasp of surprise.

He'd heard of the Jedi, of course, but everyone knew they were long extinct.

Yet somehow the boy possessed the weapon of a Jedi, even fancied *himself* a Jedi, despite the fact that he could barely strike a blow without falling on his face. There was strength there, X-7 knew, but it was well hidden, buried so deep that Luke might never find it.

The boy was too innocent, too trusting, and this, too, was something that X-7 could use. While X-7 suspected Han Solo might be persuaded to sell his information for the right price, Luke might offer it up for free.

Either could easily prove to be the weak link he needed.

Yes, someone on this ship would lead him straight to the being who had destroyed the Death Star. It was only a matter of time.

We have to decide *now*," Leia said. "We've waited long enough."

Luke sank into the copilot's chair, flinching at Chewbacca's growled warning. "I'm not trying to take your place," he assured the Wookiee. "I just need to sit down." He'd been doing calisthenics for the last couple hours. He wasn't sure if driving himself to the point of exhaustion was part of being a Jedi Knight.

But if so, he was on the right track.

"I'm don't know what the problem is," Luke said. "Elad's regained his strength, and he'd be a real asset to the mission. I say we put down on Muunilinst tonight."

"And *I* say, we know very little about him," Leia pointed out. "We have no cause to trust him, much less involve him in Rebel business. Even if he wanted to be involved."

Elad was asleep on the other side of the ship, and they'd decided to take advantage of the moment to discuss how to proceed. Luke was tired of wasting time in orbit around Muunilinst. The Rebellion needed them to *act*, not sit around and endlessly debate.

"He obviously has no love for the Empire," Luke said. "He blasted that TIE right out of the sky." He looked curiously at Leia. "Maybe if you weren't always avoiding him, you'd see that he's on our side."

"I'm not *avoiding* him," she said hotly. "I just don't know that he can be trusted. After all, he is a civilian."

Han nodded — then scowled. "Hey, *I'm* a civilian!" he protested.

Leia favored him with a cool stare. "My point exactly."

"He doesn't have a ship," Luke pointed out. "We can't just dump him into space."

"We've been over this," Leia said. "We can drop him on Destrillion — it's not too far out of our way."

"Or we could bring him with us," Luke said. "If we run into trouble, we might be glad we did."

"Or we might be betrayed at the worst possible moment," Leia argued. "You heard General Dodonna, Luke. The Empire is searching for us — for *you*. This isn't the time to take chances."

She's always trying to protect *me*, Luke thought, frustrated. Why did no one seem to understand that he

93

could protect himself? "Maybe this isn't the time to play it safe."

R2-D2 beeped and whistled.

"Yes, yes, Artoo, I'll tell them," C-3PO said irritably. "Princess Leia, Artoo says that he's run a remote search of the Malano III computer system and has confirmed Tobin Elad's identity."

The R2 droid beeped again.

"Artoo says —" C-3PO turned to him in horror. "Did you say *criminal*?" the droid asked in a panicky voice. "Artoo reports that Tobin Elad is a *wanted criminal* — the Empire has a price on his head!" His golden arms fluttered in terror. "Princess Leia, I must agree with you on this issue. The man is clearly a danger to us all. Just imagine, Artoo — trapped in space with a criminal!"

"Threepio, according to the Empire, we're *all* criminals," Luke pointed out wearily. "Even you."

"*Me*?" C-3PO asked in indignation. "I beg to differ, Master Luke. Need I remind you, I am familiar with the law of the land, and never has a droid had deeper respect for —"

"Enough!" Han exploded. "We get it. The only thing we're in danger of around you is boring ourselves to death."

"Forgive him, Threepio," Leia said, glaring at Han. "The only language he speaks is *brute*." She turned to

Luke, softening her tone. "Luke, I've heard that the Jedi were able to sense whether someone could be trusted or not. I know you're not trained . . . but can you give us anything to go on? Some kind of Jedi feeling?"

Han snorted. "You want to base a decision like this on some kooky mystical *feeling*?" he asked incredulously. "For all you know, 'Jedi feelings' were just indigestion."

"They were *not*," Luke said hotly, fully aware that he knew almost as little about the Jedi as Han. "The Jedi could see a being's true self."

At least, that's how Ben had made it sound. Luke tightened his jaw. It didn't matter what the Jedi could do . . . Han was right. *He* couldn't do anything. And without Ben around to train him, that would never change.

"Luke has a connection to the Force," Leia said fiercely. "We've all seen it." She rested a hand on top of his. "Just think about it for a moment. Do you sense *anything*?"

Luke closed his eyes. He breathed in deeply, then let the air out slowly. He tried to connect to the galaxy. *The Force is all around me,* he reminded himself. *I just have to reach for it and it will be there.*

But he felt nothing.

When he opened his eyes, Han and Leia were staring at him — Leia's eyes filled with hope, Han's with barely concealed mockery. Luke couldn't stand to be laughed at yet again.

"I think we can trust him," he said finally. "We should take him to Muunilinst with us." Maybe his opinion wasn't informed by the Force. But so what? Ben had told him to trust his instincts. For the moment, instincts would have to be enough.

Leia looked thoughtful. "I suppose Elad did sacrifice himself to help us . . ."

"Give me a break, princess," Han said in disgust. "You're *buying* this Jedi mumbo jumbo?"

"I'm just saying that maybe I was too hasty to distrust the man."

"Sure, now that —"

"Excuse me," Luke said, standing up. He knew their argument could continue indefinitely — and he suddenly felt the very strong need to be alone. He was grateful for his friends, but they couldn't understand what it was like, knowing a great power inside of him might remain hidden forever.

"Come on, Ben, where are you!" Luke exclaimed in frustration. He was sitting on the edge of his bunk, his eyes closed, intently trying to connect with Obi-Wan's spirit. The Jedi had spoken to him when he truly needed it. Surely it could happen again.

Unless that was just my imagination. Much as he tried to suppress the thought, it kept popping up.

Because if Obi-Wan Kenobi really had the power to speak from beyond the grave, why was he staying silent?

Maybe he decided I wasn't worthy of being a Jedi after all.

"Am I disturbing you?" Tobin Elad said from the doorway.

Luke opened his eyes. "No. I was just . . . doing nothing."

Elad stepped into the cramped cabin and looked around. "Are you alone in here? I thought I heard you talking to someone."

Luke flushed and shook his head. "No. I'm on my own. Come on in." He hadn't had much of a chance to talk to Elad one-on-one. This would be a good opportunity to investigate the man's motives. The Force might not be able to tell Luke whether to trust him, but that didn't mean Luke couldn't figure it out for himself.

Elad perched on a narrow counter and fixed Luke with a steady gaze. "So, have you all made your decision yet?"

"Our decision?"

"Whether to trust me." Elad smiled. "That's why we're flying around in circles, right?"

"Oh. I, uh . . ." Luke hesitated, unsure what to say.

Elad laughed softly. "It's okay — I wouldn't trust me either, if I were you. Trusting too quickly is a good way to get dead."

"So I've heard." Luke wondered if Han realized how much he and Elad had in common.

"So why aren't you up in the cockpit with the others, trying to decide my fate?"

Luke shrugged. "I had some things I needed to do."

"Lightsaber practice?" Elad asked.

Automatically, Luke's hand moved to the lightsaber hanging from his belt. It was strange how after such a short time, it had already come to feel a part of him.

"I've never met a Jedi before," Elad said. "It's quite an honor."

"I'm not a Jedi," Luke admitted. "Not yet." *Maybe not ever.*

"Well, you have the right weapon," Elad said. "That's a start."

"A lightsaber's not a weapon," Luke said, echoing what Ben had told him. "It's a tool, to focus the Force. That's what it *really* means to be a Jedi. You have to connect to the Force."

"And you don't?"

Luke ducked his head. "Not yet. Sometimes I'm afraid I never will." He'd never admitted this to Han or Leia, but somehow, it was easier to speak his concerns out loud to a stranger. "Ben — my teacher — I guess he saw something in me. He was so confident I would learn. But now he's gone. And sometimes I wonder . . . what if he was wrong?"

"You've never felt the Force?" Elad asked.

"Once," Luke admitted. "When it really counted. Everything rested on my shoulders, and I should have been terrified, but instead, I was just *certain* that I could do it. I knew it was our only chance and when I —" He cut himself off abruptly. What was he doing, talking about the Death Star with an outsider? He knew better — and this conversation was supposed to be about *Elad*. How had he ended up revealing so much about himself?

Elad looked at him curiously. "When you . . ." he prompted.

Luke shook his head. "It just felt good to save the day," he admitted. "I know I could be of much more use to the Rebellion if I could access my Jedi skills, but without Ben . . ."

Elad raised his eyebrows. "I don't know who this Ben was, but it seems to me that you don't need him to tell you how to become a Jedi. Not if he was right, and you've really got it inside of you."

"But how am I supposed to figure it out on my own?" Luke asked, feeling helpless.

"Kid, we've all got to figure it out on our own."

Luke hated it when Han called him "kid," but this

was different. When Elad said it, he somehow managed to sound like he was treating Luke as an equal.

"Every person on this ship is alone in the galaxy," Elad continued. "The Empire has seen to that."

"We're not alone if we have each other," Luke argued.

"I don't know about you," Elad said, "but sometimes I feel most alone around other people." He paused, looking like he was trying to decide whether to say more. "It's hard, having no anchor to the past, no one guiding you to the future. I know. You've just got to accept it. Stop waiting for this Ben to tell you what you want to do — find a way to decide for yourself. Something tells me you will."

The confidence in his voice spilled over into Luke. For the first time in a long time, he began to hope that he might find his way to the Jedi path all on his own. He looked up at Elad in gratitude, realizing that even without the help of the Force, his instincts had been correct.

This man was on his side.

CHAPTER TWELVE

The gray, hulking Golan III defense platform seemed to cast a shadow across space as the *Millennium Falcon* sailed slowly past.

"You *sure* these landing codes will get us through?" Han asked again, casting a glance at the turbolasers protruding from the orbiting defense station. "Because if they don't, this mission of yours is over before it starts. Along with our lives."

"They'll work," Leia said. "General Dodonna assured me."

Luke admired her certainty. Her faith in the Rebel Alliance never flagged. It was as rock solid as her loyalty and her determination. He wondered if she'd ever experienced a true moment of doubt.

As they neared the atmosphere, the Imperial official manning the spaceport called in with a request for their authorization. Leia read off the landing code she'd been given.

There was a pause.

"One moment, please," the Imperial said tonelessly.

Luke and Han exchanged a nervous glance. "Now's when they start shooting," Han predicted.

"Permission to land granted," the official informed them.

Han broke into a wide grin. "See? What'd I tell you — piece of cake."

Luke gaped wide-eyed at the towering marble columns looming over the crowded streets of Pilaan, one of Muunilinst's largest cities. Rising hundreds of stories above his head, they disappeared into a swirling mist of gray clouds.

"They don't call it Moneyland for nothing," Han said, his eyes drinking in the precious gems encrusted in several of the buildings' edifices.

"That's Money*lend*," Leia corrected him. "Nearly every wealthy being in the galaxy owes some portion of his fortune to the Muuns. It's the only reason the Empire tolerates them."

It was well-known that the Emperor considered nonhuman beings to be second-class citizens, unworthy of the privileges of Galactic power. But he made an exception for the Muuns. Although the Muun-controlled InterGalactic Banking Clan had long since been dissolved, Muunilinst retained its power as the financial center of the universe, and the Muuns remained in control.

With a heavy Imperial presence to ensure they didn't misbehave. Luke fixed his eyes on the sidewalk as they passed by a line of stormtroopers standing guard over one of the elaborate marble temples.

"Just act like you belong, kid," Han advised him. "No one will look twice."

Luke had worried they would make a strange group: four humans, two droids, and a Wookiee. But the crowded streets were filled with beings of all kinds, and no one seemed curious about any of the others. The Muuns themselves were especially unconcerned. Tall and slender, with ashy gray skin, they stood stiffly erect, their faces expressionless. It was as if they were made of marble as well.

Luke could overhear them murmuring to each other as they passed, a confusing language of short, repetitive sounds. It sounded like a world of R2 droids.

He knew he was drawing attention to himself, gaping at everything they passed, but he couldn't help it. He'd been on so few planets in his life, and all of them had housed more animals than people. Yavin 4 was nearly uninhabited, and despite its small cities, Tatooine's empty stretches of sand often seemed to stretch on forever.

This city, its streets pulsing with noise and color, its millions of inhabitants shuffling up and down the pavements, landspeeders jamming the streets, airspeeders streaking overhead — it was unlike anything he'd ever seen.

After all, not long ago, he'd been an isolated farm boy in the middle of nowhere, staring up at the stars and wondering if he would ever reach them. Now he was on the other side of the galaxy, on a secret mission in the heart of Imperial space.

Life had become infinitely more dangerous, but at the same time, infinitely more interesting. He couldn't imagine going back.

Except back then, Uncle Lars and Aunt Beru were still alive, he thought. *Shouldn't I want to go back to that old life with them? Even if it's not possible, shouldn't I wish that it were?*

Before he could let himself answer the question, they'd arrived at the rendezvous point.

"Mak Luunim lives on the twenty-third floor," Leia said, leading them to a turbolift just inside the grand white building. Even Han paused to appreciate the golden fountain glimmering at the center of the marble-encrusted lobby. But Leia was completely unfazed by the luxury.

Tobin Elad followed close behind her, seeming just as unconcerned by the surroundings.

If possible, the twenty-third floor was even more opulent than the lobby they'd left behind. The turbolift opened into a small entry area, filled with marble statues, all of the same Muun.

"My master." A sallow-faced Muun appeared behind them, seemingly from nowhere. He was dressed in a simple robe of gray and brown, his gaze fixed on the sculptures. "The great Mak Luunim. He commissioned work from Muunilinst's finest artisans, and naturally, they were all inspired to turn their talents to his noble form."

"*Naturally,*" Han muttered. "I'm sure their commission had nothing to do with it."

Leia shot him a look, its meaning clear: *Behave.*

"We have an appointment with your master," Leia told him. "He should be expecting us."

The Muun hung his head and passed his fingers along the wall. A hidden entryway opened in the marble. "You are to come inside."

They stepped into a wide parlor, squinting in the reflected glare. Dancing points of light shimmered from crystalline chandeliers, bouncing off golden walls and floor. Mak Luunim's apartment had nothing of the elegant beauty of the streets of Pilaan. Golden statuettes and framed, gilded paintings crowded nearly every inch of surface space. Even the furniture contained more gold than fabric.

Artistic representations of Mak Luunim's face gazed back at them from every wall.

"Should we wait here for your master?" Leia asked.

Luke hoped the Muun would arrive soon. He was beginning to feel deeply uncomfortable. What kind of being would choose to live like this?

"I have no master," the Muun said mournfully.

"But you said Luunim was your master," Luke pointed out, confused. Something felt off, and he was beginning to realize it wasn't just the furniture.

"Indeed," the Muun said. "Was my master. Is no more. The noble Mak Luunim has left us."

"Left us to go to the store?" Han asked hopefully. "Because we can wait."

"Left our mortal realm." The Muun's long face seemed to grow even longer as his mouth stretched in a sigh of sorrow.

Luke's hand crept toward his lightsaber.

Han frowned. "Princess, maybe we should —"

"How did he die?" Leia asked. "And when?"

"We'll ask the questions here," a voice said from behind them. Luke whirled around. The door they'd entered through was gone, turned back into solid marble. And standing in front of it, blasters drawn, was a line of six Imperial stormtroopers.

CHAPTER THIRTEEN

What business do you have with Mak Luunim?" one of the stormtroopers asked through his voice intercom.

"Who?" Han asked innocently. "Must have the wrong apartment. Now, I'm not saying all Muuns look alike, but just between you and me —"

"*State your business,*" the stormtrooper repeated, raising his blaster. Han did some quick calculations. They were surrounded, outgunned, outnumbered.

His kind of odds.

"Looks like we're done with the sweet talk portion of the evening," Han muttered under his breath. He exchanged a look with Tobin Elad, who nodded and inched toward the closest guard. *Good*, Han thought. The man knew how to read a room.

"Come quietly for detainment," the stormtrooper informed them. "Otherwise we'll shoot you right here."

"Death now or death later?" Han mused, readying his blaster. "What's behind door number three?" He pretended to think for a moment. "Oh, that's right," he added. "*Fire.*"

Elad aimed a lightning-fast kick at the nearest storm-trooper, who went down in a clatter of armor. The others guards turned in his direction, distracted just for a moment. Long enough. Han unleashed a burst of blaster fire at the troopers, then dived behind a couch before they could retaliate.

Luke and Leia fled to opposite corners, whipping out their blasters as they ran. Their fire provided enough cover for Han to take his time, aiming for the cracks in the stormtrooper armor. One by one, the Imperials went down.

The opulent apartment quickly turned into a war zone. Blaster fire tore through satin upholstery; statues of Mak Luunim blew up in a hail of marble dust. Chewbacca snarled as one of the stormtroopers tried to knock him out with a blaster to the head. He hoisted the soldier over his head and flung him through a wall separating the parlor from the dining area.

"No, no, no!" Luunim's servile employee sniveled, distraught. He ignored the blaster fire and scurried back and forth across the apartment, steadying wobbling golden vases and tossing himself across priceless heirlooms. "The master wouldn't like this at all!"

The master probably doesn't like being dead much, either, Han thought, shoving the Muun out of the way just before a burst of blaster fire could slam into him. *Sometimes you don't have a choice.*

"And *stay* down," Han advised the Muun, who had curled up beneath a coffee table, clutching a shimmering silver figurine to his chest. The creature had clearly set them up for an ambush, but that didn't mean he deserved to die.

Elad suddenly swiveled around, aiming his blaster directly at Han's head. "Hey —" Han shouted — just as the blaster fire seared past his face. There was a cry of pain from behind him as a stormtrooper took the hit.

"You're welcome," Elad smirked.

"Next time you could just say 'behind you,'" Han grumbled. But he was grateful for the save. He had to admit, Elad was just as good with a blaster as he was with a ship. He fought like a machine, cool and efficient.

Deadly.

Speaking of machines . . .

"What are you doing?" he shouted at R2-D2, almost tripping over the droid. "Figure out a way to get that door open again!"

R2-D2 beeped indignantly, but he rolled toward

the door, injecting a manipulator arm into the instrument panel.

Smoke clouded the air, heavy with the acrid stench of blaster fire. Half the stormtroopers were down, but three more crouched behind a toppled chair and table. Every few seconds, they popped up from behind their makeshift barricade and unleashed another volley of fire. Han and Elad were pinned behind a thick marble column. There was too much cover in the room, and too little space — it was impossible for Han to get a clear shot without exposing himself.

The fight was a draw . . . at least until the stormtroopers called in reinforcements.

Which could happen any minute.

"How we coming with those doors?" Han asked urgently. How long could it take to pry open some millionaire's front door?

Then again — Han took a look around the ruined apartment, realizing there was probably more wealth between these four walls than he'd smuggled in his lifetime. It was understandable that Luunim would have wanted a state of the art system to keep people out.

Or keep people in.

R2-D2 trilled triumphantly as the doors slid open.

"Go!" Elad shouted, a second before Han was about to do the same. "I'll cover you."

The droids rushed out first, followed by Leia, Luke, and Chewbacca.

"Go!" Elad shouted again, pinning down the stormtroopers with another round of fire.

"You go!" Han insisted. "I'll cover *you*."

"You want to fight about this, or you want to live?"

"You have to ask?" Han grinned.

"On three?"

Han nodded, counting silently.

One . . . two . . . three, he mouthed, and they both took off for the door, twisting backward as they ran, firing at the stormtroopers who followed. As blaster fire punched holes in the marble wall, they slipped out of the apartment, just as the doors shut behind them.

"Can you stop them from coming through?" Han asked the astromech droid.

R2-D2 whistled a response.

C-3PO looked at him in surprise. "He says he's already done so, Captain Solo. He jammed the command circuitry. Who told you to do that, Artoo?"

R2-D2 beeped and whistled, sounding proud.

"What do you mean, you came up with it on your own?" C-3PO asked, horrified. "Need I remind you of our place, Artoo? We're to carry out orders, not concoct crazy schemes sure to —"

"Nice work, Artoo," Luke cut in, smiling. "You saved us all."

"Well . . . yes, now that you mention it," C-3PO blustered, "I suppose we did."

CHAPTER
FOURTEEN

They slipped safely out of the building, quickly absorbed by the dense crowds. Leia led them up and down packed streets, wandering aimlessly in hopes of losing any Imperials that might be on their trail. But as nearly an hour passed without incident, they decided that they were safe.

For now.

They eventually found themselves on the fringes of the city. There were no more gleaming marble edifices here, only squat stone buildings the color of mud. Orange dragon beasts, nearly as large as a human foot, scampered through the streets, nibbling at the piles of garbage that lay piled on every corner. It was obvious that none of the wealthier Muuns, with their rich satin robes and fat bank accounts, ever strayed toward this part of town.

"We need to figure out why the Imperials killed Mak Luunim," Leia said, stumbling over a narrow ditch. Luke reached out to steady her, but Elad was faster. He caught her arm just before she fell. She shook him off. "If they discovered his connections to the Alliance, we could be in danger."

"Princess, those stormtroopers back there nearly turned us into burnt mealbread toast," Han pointed out. "I'd say we're already in danger."

"We need to ask around, find out whatever we can about Luunim," Luke suggested.

Han shook his head. "We *need* to lay low."

"Might I suggest a way of doing both?" Tobin Elad paused in front of a dingy cantina, its blinking sign hanging precariously over the door. So much mud spotted the windows that the transparisteel had turned a uniform brown.

"Ah, my kind of place." Han nodded appreciatively.

"*This*?" Leia wrinkled her nose and jerked out of the way as a grunting Gamorrean pushed through the doorway, his stench trailing behind him like a shadow. "It's a total dump!"

Han broke into a wide grin. "Exactly."

The inside of the cantina was even dingier than the outside. It took several minutes for their eyes to adjust to the darkness. Leia almost would have preferred it if they hadn't. Then she wouldn't have had to watch the

Gungan on the next stool brushing his companion's hair with a long, pink tongue. Or the unusually scruffy Muun behind the bar serve her a glass of water that he'd just used to wash his feet.

But in addition to clean feet, the Muun had a big mouth, and that was serving them well.

"That gundark-face Luunim owed me money," Han lied, leaning toward the bartender like they were old friends. "Should've known he'd rather die than pay me back."

"Luunim owed everyone money," the bartender said. His voice was nearly a hiss. "It was bound to get him into trouble one day." The bartender had confided that Mak Luunim died when his airspeeder's central turbine failed in midair. An Imperial inquest had deemed the incident an accident. The bartender sneered at anyone gullible enough to believe it.

"Thing is, who's going to pay me now?" Han complained. "Imperials are crawling all over the place, and I get the sense they're not too interested in paying his debts."

"Imperials!" The bartender spit into his glass. Leia resolved to keep an eye on it, lest he try to serve it to her next. "Only honorable beings repay their debts. The Imperials merely take and take — and then move on." He snickered. "Lucky thing for Nal Kenuun that he always takes first."

Han tensed, and Leia could tell he was trying his best to sound casual. "So this Nal Kenuun guy got at Luunim's place before the Imperials showed up?" Han asked. "Did Luunim owe him, too?"

"Everyone owes Nal Kenuun," the bartender said. "I have no doubt he collected on his debt, whether or not Luunim was alive to pay him."

Han glanced at Leia, and she knew exactly what he was thinking. If this Nal Kenuun had plundered Luunim's apartment, looking for items of value, then it was possible he had possession of the Rebellion's data-card — or at least might know where to find it.

Certainly it was the best lead they had, since they couldn't very well go back to Luunim's apartment and look for themselves. Not with the Empire swarming all over it.

"Don't suppose you know where I could find this Kenuun," Han said.

The bartender stiffened. "I wouldn't know anything about that." He scooped their glasses off the counter and retreated into a back room. "I got dishes to wash. Leave your payment on the counter when you go."

"That Muun never washed a dish in his life," Leia said, glancing at the spotted glasses littering the bar.

"He was definitely spooked when we started talking about Kenuun," Han agreed. "Must mean we're on the right track."

It could, in fact, have meant anything, but Leia decided not to mention that. She wanted to believe that Han was right. Because they needed that datacard — the *Rebellion* needed that datacard. And this was their only lead.

Unfortunately, the bartender wasn't the only one who refused to help. They split up, wandering into different areas of the cantina, casually dropping Nal Kenuun's name into conversations. Each conversation ended abruptly.

When they met up again outside the front door, they were no closer to Kenuun than when they'd started.

"He's rich, he's powerful, and he likes to gamble," Luke reported. "And no one wants to cross him. That's all I found out."

"Looks like that's all any of us found out," Leia said, defeated. She supposed they could return to the city center and track him down through the central directory, but with the Imperials on their tail, that seemed too great a risk.

A loud hiss slipped out of the alley behind the bar.

They fell silent, turning as one toward the source of the noise. A scaly Dug emerged from the shadows. "Yeah, you," he whispered, curling a finger toward them. "C'mere."

Chewbacca growled softly.

"I know," Han muttered. "I saw him too. Sitting alone. Watching us."

"Limited time offer," the Dug warned, retreating further into the alley.

C-3PO raised a finger in protest. "I must say, I find it highly unadvisable to follow this being into — wait, where are you all going?"

Leia led the way.

The Dug was shorter than most of his kind, barely a meter high. His scaly flesh hung thick and loose around his neck. He wore a scooped metal blade in a holster slung across his shoulders.

"Hear you're looking for Nal Kenuun," he said in a low, gravelly voice.

"It's possible." Han kept a hand on his blaster.

"Whadya want with him?" The Dug squinted with suspicion.

"Looking for some action," Han said. "Hear he's the place to get it. I've got some credits to burn."

"You think you're some kind of gambler?" the Dug asked.

"The best kind," Han retorted. "The winning kind."

"No one wins against Nal Kenuun."

Han shrugged. "Only one way to find out."

"Kenuun runs a high stakes game," the Dug warned him. "The buy-in's at ten thousand. No IOUs. You don't look like you have that kind of cash on you."

"Looks can be deceiving," Han said. "I have what I need."

Leia shot him a sharp glance. Between them, they barely had ten credits, much less ten thousand — not to mention that posing as a high-stakes gambler didn't seem to qualify as lying low.

"And what's in it for me?" the Dug asked.

"The deep pleasure of helping out a friend?" Han suggested.

The Dug snorted.

"Okay then, a hundred credits," Han said. "But only when we reach Kenuun."

Leia expected the Dug to ask for payment up front — but surprisingly, he agreed.

"Call me Grunta," he said, drawing back his thick, weathered lips into a puckered smile. "It'd be my pleasure to take you where you need to go. *Friend*." The Dug jerked his wrinkled head at the others, his ear fins twitching. "What about them?"

Han leaned in close and lowered his voice. "You know how it is when you start racking up the credits. Plenty of hangers-on wanting a piece of the action. Follow me around everywhere, do whatever I say. They're harmless."

Leia fumed, but kept her mouth shut. The Dug set off down the alley on his long, spidery forelimbs, without waiting for them to follow.

"What makes you think we can trust him?" Leia murmured to Han, as they hurried after him.

"Relax, princess," Han said. "You're in my world now."

Leia sighed. "That's what I'm afraid of."

CHAPTER FIFTEEN

The galaxy was filled with so many strange beings, Luke marveled, as they followed Grunta through a network of grungy, narrow alleys. He tried to imagine what it might be like to be a Dug, eating with his feet and walking on his hands, but it was no use. Not a surprise, Luke thought. He could barely imagine what it was like to be someone like Han, much less an alien from the other side of the galaxy.

"Seems we're going from the middle of nowhere to the edge of nowhere," Elad said lightly, falling into step with him. He didn't sound worried, just mildly curious. Han and Leia were following closely behind the Dug, with Chewbacca and the droids bringing up the rear. Luke felt an odd jolt of pleasure that Elad had chosen to speak with him. The pilot sometimes seemed so oddly removed — he smiled and laughed at all the right moments, but there was always something about him that seemed absent, as if a part of him was missing.

Maybe it is, Luke thought, remembering what Leia had told him about Elad's past. It must be hard for him to connect to people, after all he'd lost.

"So, Luke, how'd you end up with this motley crew in the first place?" Elad asked.

It seemed an odd question to ask out of the blue. "Why?"

"Just wondering." Elad shrugged. "You said you were from Tatooine, right? That's kind of a backwater — no offense."

Luke shook his head. "Trust me, I know. It's the *definition* of nowhere."

"And you're young, untrained . . . yet Leia puts so much faith in you."

"She does?" Luke asked, hoping he didn't sound as eager as he felt. He was surprised by Elad's words. Often he wondered if Leia had any faith in him at all. After all, it had been a long time since he'd done anything to deserve it.

"Sure. You can tell by the way she looks to you for advice, the way she listens. She trusts you. You've known her for a long time?"

"Not really," Luke said. "I only joined the Rebellion recently."

"But before the destruction of the Death Star, right?" Elad asked.

Luke stiffened. "You heard about that?"

Elad spit out a laugh. "The whole *galaxy* heard about that. Such a blow for freedom!" He shook his head. "I'll tell you, if I could meet the being who flew that ship . . ." He turned to Luke. "Well, you must have met him, right? Tell me, what was it like, coming face-to-face with the hero of the Rebellion?"

The hero of the Rebellion? Luke wanted nothing more than to admit the truth. Imagine, a man like Elad, admiring *him*.

But that would be against protocol.

"Never met him," Luke lied. "The Alliance is pretty big."

"Of course. I'm sure only people at the princess's level can keep track of everyone."

"Uh huh," Luke said absently, barely listening. He stopped walking. A strange feeling had swept over him.

The Force! he realized suddenly. It was warning him of something. Something evil.

Elad?

It seemed impossible. But something was definitely wrong. Elad was asking something, but Luke could barely make out the words. The air around him had become a dense, viscous fluid, making it difficult to breathe, impossible to speak or move. Everything was now darkness.

And then, without warning, the feeling of doom vanished. Light returned to the world.

"Hey, you okay, kid?" Han asked. The whole group was staring at him, like he'd had some kind of fit.

"Fine." Luke drew in a few deep, even breaths. He glanced at Elad, whose concern looked just as sincere as everyone else's.

But was it?

Luke shook off their questions. "I just got dizzy for a second. Must have been the sun. Or maybe —"

An explosion of blaster fire drowned out his words. Grunta had opened fire on them!

Chewbacca lunged for the Dug, knocking the blaster out of his hands. But a thunder of engines rumbled overhead. Four swoops streaked toward them, all piloted by Dugs, their blasters drawn.

It was an ambush.

So this *is what the Force was warning me about,* Luke thought, furious with himself. *If only I'd understood, rather than wasting time worrying about Elad.* His hand flew automatically to his lightsaber, but then hesitated.

Han was right: What good was a weapon he didn't know how to use?

He pulled out his blaster instead, and returned fire.

It may have been a surprise attack, but this time, they were neither outgunned nor outnumbered. They were, however, at a serious disadvantage. The Dugs swooped in and out of range at will.

Luke and his friends stood in a tight clump, their backs to each other, their blasters aimed at the sky as the Dugs circled overhead.

"All we want is the money!" Grunta shouted over the roar of the engines. Chewbacca had wrestled him to the ground. He flailed about wildly, trying to wound the Wookiee with his sharp blade. "Give us that and you're free to go."

"Maybe we should tell them we don't have any money," Luke said quietly.

Han snorted. "Great idea. I'm sure they'll wish us a happy afternoon and send us on our way."

"You have a better idea?" Leia retorted. "After all, your plans have been working so beautifully today."

"I don't know about better, but —" Han pulled a sack from beneath his coat and waved it in the air. "You want the credits?" he shouted. "Come and get 'em!" The swoop dived toward the ground, a spindly Dug arm reaching out for the empty sack. Han dropped the bag and grabbed the arm instead, yanking hard. "Now, kid!" he yelled, as the Dug toppled off the swoop.

Without thinking, Luke took a flying leap for the

swoop. It was farther and faster than he should have been able to jump — but somehow, he made it.

The Force, he thought gratefully, gripping the controls and pivoting around so that Han could clamber aboard behind him. He took off after one of the other Dugs, who rocketed upward in a steep vertical climb, then suddenly broke into a corkscrew dive. Luke followed, accelerating as they plummeted downward, zooming in so close that the Dug's exhaust warmed his face. Han aimed over Luke's shoulder and launched a blast at the starboard engine. It blazed white hot, then exploded, a shower of fiery durasteel fragments raining down on them. As Luke ducked and weaved to avoid the flying shrapnel, the Dug's swoop dropped out of the sky. Luke pulled up seconds before crashing into the ground, and spiraled upward toward the next speeder.

"Who's next?!" Han shouted gleefully.

The three remaining Dugs took one look at what remained of their friend, and decided they'd rather be alive and poor than rich and dead. The swoops took off toward the city center, disappearing into the skyline. Luke brought his swoop back to the ground. "Nice flying, kid," Han said. "Couldn't have done it better myself." A moment later, Han reconsidered. "Well, I could've. But no one else."

Back at ground level, Leia, Elad, and Chewbacca surrounded the wreckage of the fallen speeder.

"Where's Grunta?" Luke asked, looking around.

Chewbacca growled, and pointed a hairy finger at the crashed speeder. On closer inspection, Luke spotted a scaly Dug arm poking out from beneath the wreckage.

Elad grinned. "I *said* 'heads up.' Guess he didn't hear me."

"Now what?" Luke asked, feeling deflated as the rush of battle adrenaline leaked out of him. "We're right back where we started."

"Simple," Han said confidently. "We just have to . . ." His voice trailed off, as a strange, queasy expression came over his face. "I've got a bad feeling about . . ." He dropped to the ground, unconscious.

"Han!" Leia rushed to his side — but froze just before she reached him. She looked up, a puzzled expression on her face. Then she toppled to the ground.

"Poison darts," Elad said, tilting his head to look for a sniper in one of the buildings that rose above them. "We should —" Without warning, he dropped. Chewbacca followed a moment later, with a growl and a deafening thud.

Duck! The command seemed to come from within, but Luke obeyed it. As he did, a dart whizzed past, skimming his hair as it blew by.

"That was close, Master Luke," C-3PO said worriedly. "We must seek cover before —"

Luke darted to his left, just as another dart streaked

past. Something, his instincts, his senses — *the Force?* — was warning him of the danger a split second before it arrived. But he couldn't dodge darts indefinitely. He had to find a way to help his friends.

They're just unconscious, he assured himself, looking away from their still bodies and pale faces. *They can't be —*

"You're a quick one," a voice said from behind him. Luke whirled around to find himself face-to-face with a white-armored face mask. "Not quick enough."

The stormtrooper raised a force pike and jabbed him in the chest. Luke's body shuddered uncontrollably as the electric shock blazed through him. There was an explosion of pain, and his legs collapsed beneath him.

The massive shock paralyzed his nervous system. He lay on his back, unable to move, staring up at the stormtrooper. Helpless.

Luke prepared himself to die.

The force pike struck again.

More pain.

And then, only darkness.

Luke opened his eyes. It was pitch-black. Binders around his wrists held his arms above his head. Similar bolts wrapped around his waist and ankles, pinning him against a cool stone wall.

Everything hurt.

He struggled against the restraints, but they held fast. There was no hope of reaching his lightsaber, which, as the world came back into focus, he saw was still attached to his belt. No hope of escape. Luke tried not to panic.

He was a Jedi, he reminded himself. He should be able to *think* his lightsaber into his hand. But he had no idea how to do so.

"Take it easy, kid," Han's voice floated out of the darkness. "Your eyes will adjust soon enough."

Chewbacca yowled from a few feet away. Luke

thought he could make out a hulking shadow that might have been the Wookiee.

"Of course he's all right," Han said. "I wasn't worried."

Chewbacca growled something back.

"Only because it took him so long to wake up!" Han said defensively. "It's not my fault he has a weak constitution."

"Hey!" Luke protested feebly. The lingering effects of the force pike made his muscles feel like jelly. Even if he could escape from the binders, Luke feared he might not be able to stand, much less fight.

"I think we've been here for several hours," Tobin Elad said. "It's unclear what they're waiting for."

"Did the droids escape?" Luke asked. "Maybe they can help us."

"Maybe," Leia said, but she didn't sound particularly hopeful. Luke, his eyes still adjusting to the dark, peered across the room at her shadowy figure, pinned against the wall. He began struggling against the restraints again. Being trapped was bad enough. But imagining Leia dangling helplessly, while he could do nothing to save her? That was intolerable.

"Or maybe they're already scrap metal on some Imperial construction project," Han said. "Probably more pleasant than whatever's in store for us."

A door swung open, letting a shaft of bright light into the room. Luke winced at the sight of his friends chained to the walls. A trickle of dried blood ran down the side of Leia's face.

The stormtrooper's white armor gleamed. "I've been ordered to ask if you're thirsty."

"Sure," Han said. "How's about you unlock these cuffs and you and I can go grab a drink? Get to know each other a little."

The stormtrooper crossed the room, stopping inches from Han's immobilized body. Luke held his breath.

Instead of a blaster, the guard pulled out a transparent container of liquid, holding it to Han's lips. "Drink."

Han did — then spat the water in the stormtrooper's face.

For a moment, the guard didn't react. Then he pressed a button on his wrist console. Han shouted in pain as the binders around his wrists sizzled with electric current. His head dropped to his chest as he slipped into unconsciousness.

"Anyone else want a drink?" the stormtrooper asked, in a conversational tone.

Silence.

He shrugged and turned to leave the room. "Wait!" Luke shouted, a desperate plan taking shape.

The stormtrooper paused, turning to face Luke. "You want to test out your stun cuffs, too?"

Luke closed his eyes, trying to call on the Force. *I need you now, Ben*, he thought, remembering the day that Ben had first revealed himself as a Jedi Master. He'd used the Force to manipulate the minds of his enemies. *The Force can have a strong influence on the weak-minded*, Ben had said.

"You don't want to hold us prisoner anymore." Luke stared intensely at the guard. "You want to let us go."

There was a long pause.

"No I don't," the stormtrooper said. The door shut behind them, and darkness closed in again.

Hours crept by. Maybe days. There was no way to gauge the passing of time. Luke swallowed hard, his throat dry and scratchy. He wondered if the guard would ever return with more water. Or perhaps this was what the Empire had in store for them all along — a long, slow death by dehydration. They would hang here until their stomachs shrank, their bodies dried out, and they grew weaker and weaker, until they prayed for the end.

They didn't speak much. Everyone had retreated into their own thoughts. Perhaps they were formulating escape plans, but Luke doubted it.

Escape seemed hopeless.

Now there was nothing to do but wait.

Luke was asleep when the door opened again. It was the light that woke him. He squinted, unaccustomed to the brightness that filled the room. A Muun, taller and slimmer than the others they'd seen, stood in the doorway, his shimmering green robe stretching to the floor.

The Muun nodded, and the cuffs around Luke's wrists and ankles suddenly released. He tumbled to the hard floor with a painful thump. One by one, his friends dropped to the ground as well.

"Apologies for my guards," the Muun said in Basic, his nasal voice sounding unaccustomed to the vowels. "They tend to get carried away."

Luke slowly pulled himself into a sitting position. When he tried to stand, his legs nearly gave out beneath him. Finally, he forced himself upright, sagging against the wall for support. Whatever the Muun had in store for them, Luke vowed he would find the strength to fight back.

They'd been stripped of their blasters. But at least he still had his lightsaber. That was something.

"*Your* guards?" Leia asked. She, too, was leaning against the wall. Chewbacca had pulled Han into a standing position and had a furry arm around the pilot. Only Tobin Elad stood firm and upright, apparently unharmed by the ordeal. "Not the Emperor's?"

The Muun gave her a faint smile. "Even the Empire has debts to repay," he said cryptically. "Occasionally I elect to take my remuneration in a non-monetary form. Having Imperial guards in my employ can prove useful from time to time, but occasionally . . ." He shook his head. "They can be a bit *overenthusiastic*. And when that happens . . . well, I'm told you already know about Mak Luunim."

Luke exchanged a meaningful glance with Leia. So Luunim hadn't been killed by the Empire after all. Which meant his death likely had nothing to do with his connection to the Rebel Alliance.

"*You* ordered him killed?" Luke said. "Why?"

"Now, now, precision is everything," the Muun chastised him. "Muunilinst is a civilized planet — having someone killed would be a crime. But can I be held accountable for actions my guards take in their own defense?"

"We know nothing of Luunim's dealings with you," Leia said, without a single note of fear in her voice. "And we have no interest in avenging his death. We are not your enemies."

"That remains to be seen," the Muun told her. "First you show up at Luunim's dwelling. Then you masquerade as gamblers so as to track me down? You've been rather busy — and, it seems, very intent on involving yourself in my business." He smiled at the look of surprise on their faces. "Oh yes, I'm Nal Kenuun, the one you've been looking for. Now, would anyone like to explain why you continue to bother me?"

"We're bothering *you*?" Han asked incredulously. "Hey, easy solution, just let us walk out of here, we'll never bother you again."

"We came for something that belongs to us." Leia spoke over Han's blustering. "Luunim was holding a datacard of financial access codes. It's ours, and we believe you confiscated it along with the rest of his valuables. We'd like it back, please." She sounded like she was making an official request in the Senatorial chambers, rather than begging something of her captor as she cowered in his dungeon.

Kenuun nodded. "Yes, I have taken possession of Luunim's financial records. It's likely I have what you're looking for. And of course, if it belongs to you, I have no right to hold it. Except . . ."

"*Except*?" Han repeated. "*Except* is never good."

Chewbacca grumbled in agreement.

"Except that *you* took something of mine. Something of great value."

"We've taken nothing from you," Luke insisted.

"To the contrary, you took one of my most prized

possessions," Kenuun argued. "I believe you knew him by the name of Grunta?"

"That was self-defense!" Luke protested. "He ambushed us."

"I'm sure he did," Kenuun said. "Getting into trouble was one of Grunta's few talents. It's the reason I had him shadowed by a homing droid — lucky thing, or I might never have found the beings who killed him."

So the guards weren't after us, Luke thought. *They were after the Dug.*

"The Muuns are honorable beings," Kenuun said. "And I would be happy to return your possession to you — once you replace mine."

"And just how are we supposed to replace your pet Dug?" Han asked.

"By doing his job for him. Grunta may have had many failings, but he was an *excellent* Podracer. And in the Podrace two days hence, he was about to earn me a rather large sum of money."

"Podracing is illegal," Leia said. "Half the racers end up dead."

"Indeed. Poor Grunta was probably lucky to live as long as he did. And certainly this was a more pleasant way to go." The Muun crossed his long, slender arms. "Be that as it may, the race goes on. One of *you* will take Grunta's spot in the race. And you will win. I'll receive my money, you'll receive your datacard."

"How do we know you'll keep your end of the bargain?" Luke asked.

Kenuun looked offended. "I'm a *Muun*," he said. "There's nothing more sacred to my people than keeping our word in financial dealings."

"It's true," Han pointed out. "Muuns'll take you for everything you've got, but they never cheat."

"It's irrelevant," Elad snapped. "No human can win a Podrace. The best of human pilots would be lucky to even *finish* the race without crashing. And since I don't think the Wookiee is up to the task . . ."

"One of you will enter the race," Kenuun said again, unmoved. "You will win. Then and only then, the datacard will be yours."

"Unless we die trying," Han added.

The Muun nodded at the two stormtroopers who flanked him on either side. They raised their blasters, aiming them toward the prisoners. "There are many ways to die," he said serenely. "And as you knew Mak Luunim, you know what happens to beings who choose not to repay their debts to me."

"We'll do it," Luke said. "We'll race, and we'll win. We accept your bargain."

Leia shot him an alarmed look. "Have you ever *seen* a Podrace?" she asked. "It's certain death."

Luke had seen several Podraces — Tatooine was one of the few places left in the galaxy where the illegal sport still flourished. He knew that no human had the reflexes to compete. No *ordinary* human, at least.

But he also knew that they had no choice.

And that when it came to flying, he was far from ordinary.

"We'll do it," he repeated. "*I'll* do it."

CHAPTER SEVENTEEN

The dead Dug's Podracer was a top of the line Collor Pondrat Plug-2 Behemoth, with a top speed of 790 kilometers per hour. According to Nal Kenuun, it also had a modified traction system and an upgraded throttle. Its bulky engines were streaked with elaborate green and yellow flames, while the cockpit was painted an angry red, with a green "K" stenciled on either side.

Kenuun's guards had taken them to an empty, barren area a hundred kilometers outside of the city. A network of cavernous cliffs loomed to one side, while on the other, there was nothing in sight but flat, weedy ground stretching to the horizon. Tents had been erected to house the other Podracers and their crews. It would be a small, elite race, with only five other racers. They had all arrived and were pretending to studiously polish and tweak their engines. But it was obvious they were all watching the newest entrant to the race.

Luke folded himself into the narrow seat, which had been custom designed for a creature significantly shorter than he was. Leia winced as he banged his knees hard against the steering controls.

"You look like a Wookiee trying to squeeze inside a gartro nest, kid," Han joked.

Leia shushed him — but she had to admit it was true. Kenuun had given them a choice of Podracers, but all were equally unsuited for a driver of Luke's size. Podracing just wasn't designed for humans. She didn't know very much about the sport, but Elad had explained that the top racers often sped through a course at more than 900 kilometers per hour. Human reflexes weren't fast enough to take a hairpin turn at that kind of speed.

And then there was the size issue. Podracers were vehicles only in the most technical sense of the term. Leia had never seen one close up before, and she still couldn't believe this heap of loosely connected engine parts was supposed to take Luke through the racecourse. The tiny repulsorlift cockpit was connected by long, flexible cables to the two massive engines. Because the frame was so unstable, it was easily unbalanced. This was why most racers were less than one meter tall. The less weight in the cockpit, the less chance there was that the Podracer would flip over, dumping its driver.

In challenging courses, this happened to even the most experienced of drivers.

And Luke, by his own admission, had no experience at all.

"You sure you understand the controls?" Leia asked nervously, as Luke prepared to ignite the engines and take off for his first practice run. The droids stood by her side, freshly polished and buffed — Kenuun had treated them somewhat better than his human prisoners. "I'm sure one of the other Podracers would —"

"I know what I'm doing," Luke said irritably. "It's just like flying anything else, right?"

"Just hold on tight, kid," Han advised. "No need to go too fast your first time out."

Chewbacca let out a long growl.

"Well let's *hope* he knows not to do that," Han told the Wookiee. "Be a shame for him to crash before the race even starts."

Luke sighed. "I *was* the best pilot in Mos Eisley," he reminded them, shifting uncomfortably in the seat. His knees were nearly grazing his chin. "And I'm the only one of us who's actually seen a Podrace. I know what I'm doing."

Before they could say anything else, the Podracer lifted off, a violet current crackling between the engines. Luke waved, and the Podracer sped away, so fast it was soon nothing but a smear of red against the grayish sky.

The engines twisted and wobbled alarmingly as Luke struggled to maintain the balance. The cockpit swung from side to side, then dipped forward, plummeting toward the ground.

"He can't control it!" Leia gasped, peering through her electrobinoculars.

"He'll be fine," Han assured her. "The kid knows what he's doing." But he didn't sound convinced.

"I hate to suggest this," Elad said, "but it might be time to start thinking about a backup plan. If Luke can't pull this off . . ."

He was only saying what she herself had been thinking, but something in Leia rebelled at his words. "Luke is the best pilot I've ever met," she said fiercely.

"Hey!" Han protested.

"The *best*," Leia repeated. "He just needs practice. He'll be fine."

Elad raised his eyebrows. "The best you've ever met?" He peered into the distance. The Podracer's cockpit was bouncing furiously over air pockets. Thanks to his erratic steering, Luke was battling his own turbulence. "Even if he wins the race, Kenuun could still double cross us. Perhaps we should think about —"

"We'll proceed with the current plan," Leia said sharply, cutting off all further discussion. She may have let Elad accompany them on their mission, but she wasn't about to cede control. "I have faith in Luke."

The Podracer listed precariously to the right side, as it returned toward them. A burst of orange flame exploded from the right engine.

"He's overheating!" Han shouted, running toward the Podracer.

With one engine dead, steering was impossible. The Podracer shot into an out of control spin. The engines whirled wildly around the cockpit. Suddenly, the Podracer tilted vertically, and shot straight up in the air.

"Luke!" Leia cried, taking off after Han. The Podracer flipped upside down and screamed into a dive. It was still nearly a kilometer up in the air when a tiny figure toppled out of the cockpit.

An endless moment later, Luke's chute inflated. He drifted slowly to the ground. The Podracer rocketed downward, hitting the ground with a deafening crash. It exploded on impact, gushing a fiery spray of fuel and shorn metal into the air.

Luke wrapped himself in the chute and rolled away

from the crash site, trying to shield himself from the falling debris. Leia and the others had almost reached him when one of the slim, fiery strips of durasteel landed on his chute.

The parachute burst into flames.

Luke was a ball of fire. Han slapped his coat at the burning parachute, trying to smother the flames.

"Roll over!" he shouted. Luke started rolling across the dirt. Slowly — too slowly — the flames flickered out.

The parachute was an ashen, blackened mess. The body hidden beneath lay motionless.

"Luke?" Leia said quietly, her voice filled with terror. "Luke!"

He moved.

Luke threw off the charred chute. His face was sooty and his body covered by sandy abrasions, but he was alive. He stood up. "I'm okay," he said, stretching his limbs one at a time to make sure it was true. "I'm okay."

A flood of relief washed over Han. "Close one, kid," he said, trying to keep his voice light. If Luke had fallen from the Podracer any sooner, or any later ... If his chute had malfunctioned, or if the armorweave hadn't protected him from the flames ...

Did Luke understand how close he'd come to the end? Han watched as Luke's horrified gaze took in the simmering ruins of the Podracer.

He understood.

"The engine flamed out," Luke said, taking a few hesitant steps. "Must have been a defective current filter. I should have had Artoo double check it before I took off. Next time I'll know better."

"*Next time?*" Leia shook her head. "Luke, there's not going to be a next time. You almost died. The Podracer's destroyed."

"Kenuun wants to win this race — he'll give us another one," Luke said confidently.

"And is he going to give us another one of you?"

"Give him a break, princess." Han slung an arm around Luke. "The kid doesn't even know what he's saying."

Luke shrugged him off. "Yes I do. And a faulty current filter's not going to stop us from completing this mission. The Rebellion needs us to win this race."

The Rebellion needs you to live, Han thought.

But he kept his mouth shut.

*   *   *

147

Eventually, Luke got his way. Leia and Elad met with Kenuun in hopes of laying their hands on a second Podracer. The Muun had a hangar full of them — it seemed likely he'd be willing to produce another.

Han took Luke back to their makeshift campsite to rest. There were less than twenty-four hours to go before the race, and Luke knew every second counted. But he couldn't practice without a Podracer — and he had to admit, resting sounded good. His shoulder and back throbbed from the fall, and a deep series of scrapes along his back flared with pain wherever his shirt brushed the skin.

It could have been worse, he reminded himself. *Much worse.*

"Whatcha thinking?" Han asked, as they sat in front of their tent, watching the sun sink toward the horizon. A few of the Podracers swooped back and forth in the distance, getting in one more run before race day.

"I would've had it," Luke said. "I was getting control. If the engine hadn't flamed out — I would've had it."

"I know, kid," Han said.

Luke looked at him in surprise. "You do?"

Han shrugged. "Sure. Don't forget, I saw you take on the Death Star. I know what you can do."

"Maybe," Luke said. He'd been doing his best to act confident — but it was just that. An act. He had to convince the others that he could fly the Podracer. It was the only way they'd go along with the plan. But Luke had seen a Podrace. He knew how fast the racers traveled, how challenging even a familiar course could be. How even in the best of circumstances, things could go wrong.

And when things went wrong in a Podrace, they went very wrong.

"You don't have to do this, you know," Han said, as if he could hear Luke's thoughts. "I wouldn't."

"I have to," Luke said. "It's the only way. And I know I can win. At least . . . if the Force is with me."

"Just how big an 'if' are we talking here?" Han asked.

Luke drew his lightsaber. Instead of activating the beam, he just cradled the hilt in his hands. He found the heft of the cool metal comforting. A reminder of the person he was supposed to be. "I can't control it," Luke admitted. "The harder I try, the more impossible it seems."

"You know I don't think much of this Force of yours," Han began.

Luke sighed. He wasn't in the mood. "Can we just —"

"Slow down, kid," Han said. "Let me finish." He frowned at the lightsaber. "I think most of it's a bunch of mumbo jumbo, and if you ask me, that Ben of yours was a few sabacc cards short of a deck. *But —*" He held up a hand to stop Luke from interrupting again. "He was a tough old guy. And he had . . . I don't know. Call it the Force, call it whatever you want. I saw him take on Vader — and that was something."

"Something, maybe. But not enough." Luke closed his eyes for a moment, trying to block out the image of Vader's red beam striking that final, fatal blow.

"He knew what he was doing," Han said. "He could have run away, saved himself, sure. But he wasn't trying to save himself. He was trying to save *you*. And he got you off that ship."

Luke shook his head. "But that's just it. He sacrificed himself for *me*, so I could become a Jedi Knight — but I *can't!* Not without him. I can't use the Force, not when I need it. I let him down."

"So quit."

Luke scowled. "I can't do that. I'm not —" He stopped himself.

"Me?" Han smiled wryly. "Thanks for the compliment."

"I wasn't going to say that."

"Right." Han got serious. "I don't mean you should quit the fight. I mean you should quit trying so hard. Look, I may not know about this Jedi stuff, but I know ships, and I know *flying*. And what I know is that you've got to trust your ship. Let her tell you what she needs. The best pilots become part of their ships. And that's not something you *try* to do. You just do it. You've got to relax. Let it happen."

Let go of your conscious self, Ben had urged him. *Act on instinct.*

Maybe Han knew more about the Jedi way than he thought.

Han stood up, giving Luke a light slap on the back. "And when I say the best pilots, kid, I'm talking about you. Oh, one more thing."

"What?" Luke asked.

Han grinned. "Next time, try not to fall out."

an gulped down his second glass of lum. Chewbacca handed him another. They'd left Luke back at the campsite to study the map of the race circuit. Most of the other Podracers and their crew were crowded into a large tent, swigging drinks and swapping stories, and no one seemed to mind Han's presence. The noise helped drown out his thoughts.

When he'd left Luke, the kid had seemed more certain than ever that he could handle the Podrace. *Thanks to you*, he'd told Han. *Now I know I can do it.*

Han just wished he could be so sure.

And he wished that Luke had never said that: *Thanks to you*. Because now if something went wrong, Han would know exactly who to blame.

"Thought I'd find you two here," Elad said, pushing his way through the crowd to join Han and Chewbacca.

"Any luck with Kenuun?" Han asked.

"One Keizar-Volvec KV9T9-B Wasp, with a top speed of 800 km per hour and a fully functioning current filter. Luke's testing it out right now — he didn't want an audience."

Han just grunted, and took another swallow of his lum. It was watery and lukewarm, but it did the trick.

"Leia's keeping an eye on him," Elad added.

"Kid's going to be fine," Han mumbled. "We should all just relax."

Elad nodded, but said nothing.

A Phlog appeared before them, his thick, greenish finger exploring the innards of his bulbous nose. "Rumor has it, you're the folks who killed Grunta," he growled.

Elad and Han exchanged a look. Chewbacca issued a warning growl. Han knew the prudent thing to do was deny it and walk away. That's what Leia would have advised.

"Rumor's right," Han said.

The Phlog yanked his finger out of his nose, used it to stir his drink, then gulped the lum down in one shot. "Hey, these are the guys who killed Grunta!" he shouted to the crowd.

All noise and motion immediately ceased. Every face turned toward Han, Elad, and Chewbacca.

Uh oh, Han thought. But he was almost looking forward to a fight.

The crowd exploded into cheers. The Phlog slapped Han on the back and ordered another round of drinks. His treat.

"I'm guessing Grunta wasn't a friend of yours?" Han asked, starting to get the picture.

"That piece of bantha slime?" The Phlog spit out a wad of purple phlegm. It spattered on the ground inches from Han's boots. He held out a massive, sticky hand for Han to shake. "Haari Ikreme Beeerd, at your service," he said. "Any enemy of Grunta is a friend to us all."

"You a Podracer?" Elad asked.

The Phlog shook his head, gesturing at his massive bulk. He was three times the size of an average Podracer. "Crew — for Gilag Pitaaani over there." He pointed across the tent to a stubby Nuknog who was crushing a bottle of fizzbrew against his knobby skull. "We race for the Muun Chenik Kruun." Haari Ikreme unleashed a rapid string of chokes and coughs that Han suspected might be laughter. "A cold-blooded, emotionless sand snake if I ever saw one, but when he heard about Grunta's death, he nearly *smiled*. Nothing would make him happier than beating Nal Kenuun."

"My master, too," a Glymphid put in, raising a mug of lum with the suction cup at the end of one of his spindly fingers. "All these Muuns, they hate each other. But one thing unites them — they hate Kenuun more."

"And why not?" Haari Ikreme said. "A colder, crueler being you'll never meet." He sputtered with his strange laughter again. "Unless you're a krayt dragon, that is."

"And why's that?" Elad asked.

"Haven't you heard?" Haari Ikreme asked in surprise. "Everyone knows that Kenuun loves nothing in this galaxy except his baby krayt dragon. The whole planet's laughing about it behind his back. Of course, the last one foolish enough to laugh in front of him learned his lesson."

"Kenuun punished him?" Han asked.

"Killed him," the Glymphid said.

"And his family," Haari Ikreme added. "Not that anyone could prove it. No, Kenuun's smart. Just not smart enough to find himself a pilot who could actually win the race."

"You should see what he's got racing for him," the Nuknog said, chortling. "We're taking bets on how quickly the human dies. Low bid's fifty, if you want in."

Chewbacca growled. Han put a hand on his shoulder. Weapons weren't allowed inside the tent, so they'd left their blasters back at the campsite. "Easy, buddy," he murmured.

"I saw him out there this afternoon," the Glymphid jeered. "Kenuun's making a joke out of this whole race. We'll be lucky if the human doesn't take us all down with him when he goes."

Haari Ikreme leaned toward Han. "*I'll* be lucky if the human dies within the first ten kilometers," he whispered. "I've got two thousand riding on it. Cross your fingers for me."

Now it was Chewbacca who warned Han to take it easy. But Han was beyond listening to warnings. "That's our *friend* you're talking about, buddy," Han said through gritted teeth. "And he's going to make it through that race and leave you all eating dust."

Haari Ikreme and his friends burst into laughter. "You're a funny one, Grunta-killer," he gasped. "I like you!"

"No blasters," murmured Elad, as a reminder.

Han ignored him. "Oh yeah? See how you like *this*." And punched the Phlog in his squinched up, bulbous face.

The Glymphid was on top of him in seconds, grinding a small but powerful fist into Han's stomach. Elad leaped into the fray. He pulled the Glymphid off of Han and tossed him into the air.

"This your idea of relaxing?" Elad shouted, as he fended off a blow from the dazed Phlog, then pivoted around to kick a lunging Nuknog in the stomach.

"Haven't felt this relaxed in days!" Han shouted back, ducking just in time for two charging Sneevels to miss him and crash into each other. Soon every alien in the tent had entered the brawl. Kicks and punches flew wildly, bodies rolled through the dust.

Chewbacca had a Xexto and a Nuknog trapped in his mighty grasp. He roared as a Rodian broke a chair over his head. Han grabbed the Rodian by the shoulders and slammed him into the ground, leaping over his body just in time to avoid an Exodeenian's six-armed punch.

Suddenly Haari Ikreme emerged from the chaos. He was holding a blaster pistol, aimed straight at Han. "Perhaps Grunta was a better friend to me than I knew," the Phlog said. "Perhaps he needs to be avenged."

"Easy, fella," Han said, stalling. "Aren't you forgetting something? What happens when *my* friends decide to avenge me?"

The Phlog cocked his weapon. "Something tells me pulling this trigger will make me more new friends than I can count. In fact, I —"

He broke off, as a Glymphid sailed past them, slamming into the main strut holding up the tent. The strut snapped in two, toppling over and bringing the tent down on top of them with a soft sigh. Han took advantage of the distraction, knocking the blaster out of Haari Ikreme's hand. Before the Phlog could retaliate, he pushed his way through the fallen canvas, trying to find his way to the outside.

The brawl ended as the other fighters did the same, swiftly wriggling out from under the sunken tent. Han found Elad and Chewbacca, both bruised but intact.

"What do you say we get out of here," Han suggested, scanning the crowd for an angry Haari Ikreme. When it came to flash brawls like this, grudges were usually forgotten by morning.

But that was still a few hours away.

Podraces on Tatooine always drew crowds. Hundreds, even thousands of spectators, eager to watch the racers speed through the course. Even more eager to watch them crash and burn.

But here, there were no crowds.

Only the wealthiest, most elite gamblers of Muun society were given access to the secret race's location. Fewer than twenty Muuns had assembled in the deserted wilderness. Rather than exposing themselves to the day's blistering sunlight, they hovered in climate controlled transparisteel bubbles. Podrace cam droids would follow the racers through the course, beaming the images back to the Muuns' viewscreens. Wrecking crews stood by in case of a crash. There were no medical technicians. That was an expense the Muuns were unprepared to pay.

Especially since Podrace crashes rarely left survivors.

The starting point was located well outside of Pilaan, on a wide, dusty plain. In the distance loomed a rocky cliffside, split by a deep, narrow crevice. According to the map, navigating this would be the first hurdle of the race.

Not a problem, Luke told himself, waiting at the starting line. *I've got it under control.* His friends stood in a tight clump around him, all looking like they were attending a funeral. The other Podracers and their crews clustered a few feet away, staring at Luke. Han kept shooting nervous glances at a burly Phlog, but the others focused all their attention on Luke.

"Luke, I can't let you do this," Leia said in a worried voice. "What if something goes wrong again?"

But R2-D2 had checked and rechecked every inch of the Podracer. It was in full working order. If there was a failure, it wouldn't be a mechanical one.

"Nothing will go wrong," Luke said, sounding more certain than he felt. "I can win this."

"You could *die*," Leia reminded him.

Han glared at her. "Great pep talk, Your Worship."

"He doesn't need a pep talk," Leia said angrily. "He needs to hear the truth. And the truth is that he can't do this. No human can."

"It's true that statistically, Master Luke has very little

chance of surviving this course," C-3PO put in, "but in fact a full search of the galactic Podracing records has revealed a historical precedent for —"

"I don't care if no human has ever done it before," Luke interrupted. "*I* can."

"So that's what this is about?" Leia asked hotly. "You're trying to prove something?"

"I'm *trying* to help the Alliance," Luke reminded her. "And if I die today, at least I'll die trying to do what's right. Some things are more important than my life, Leia. Bigger. *You* taught me that."

"Don't throw my words back at me, to defend a stupid idea like this," Leia shouted.

"Then I won't say anything else," Luke said quietly. "You know how I feel."

Leia narrowed her eyes. "Fine. I can't stop you. But I don't have to stick around here and watch you die."

She stormed away before Luke could respond.

"Where are you going?" Han called after her. "Come back!"

Luke shook his head. "Let her go," he said quietly. "She's right. It's better if she's not here for this."

"Hey, kid, you know you're going to be okay, right?" Han asked.

Chewbacca growled in agreement.

"We believe in you," Elad added. "Leia does, too."

"I know," Luke said. "And that's all I need."

But as his friends wished him good luck and joined the other crews, Luke knew that was a lie. He climbed into the Podracer as it was towed into position at the starting line. He was alone in this. It didn't matter whether his friends believed in him.

He had to believe in himself.

Luke eyed the other racers. To his immediate right was a Glymphid, his suction-tipped fingers piloting a red brute of a Podracer. The alien shot him a cocky grin. On his other side, a knobby-headed Nuknog glowered behind the controls of his Bin Gassi Quadrijet.

Luke shifted in his seat, trying to find the best position. His too-long limbs jutted out at all angles, and he was folded into the cramped cockpit built for a much smaller being. But before Luke could get comfortable, the starting lights glowed. Red . . . Orange . . . *Green!*

Wind and gravel bit into Luke's face as he surged forward. The Podracer was like a wild animal, bucking and heaving beneath him. The world swept past in smears of blue and gray. A constant thunder of air rumbled in his ears, and the billowing dust clouds blown up by the stream of Podracers nearly blinded him. He tipped left, then pulled to the right, but overcorrected. The Podracer listed to the side, nearly overturning. Luke pulled up hard, just barely holding his balance. Three of the other racers had all whizzed past, disappearing into the dark crevice in the cliffside.

The fourth, a quad-engined Balta-Trabaat BT310 flown by a Xexto, went in at the wrong angle, and smacked its lower left engine into the side of the cliff. It exploded. Flames rippled up the cables connecting the engine to the cockpit, and a moment later, the Xexto and his Podracer burst into a ball of fire.

Luke flew erratically, struggling to gain control. He tried to catch his breath, but choked on the acrid smoke streaming from the Xexto's wreckage. The Podracer was fighting him, shuddering at his touch. The cliff drew closer, a vertical sheet of rock. His body went rigid with fear. The entrance was only a few feet wider than the Podracer. If Luke miscalculated his approach, or if the Podracer spun out of control, his race would be over nearly before it began. Along with his life.

No, he thought furiously, relaxing his grip on the controls. *Don't think about that.*

Don't think about anything.

Luke took a deep breath. The Force was out there, he reminded himself. Surrounding him. Supporting him. It filled him, as it filled his ship. He wasn't strong enough, wasn't fast enough, to gain control over the Podracer.

But maybe he could be wise enough to release it.

Luke let his instincts take over. He stopped worrying about what might happen, or about what he had to do. He let the ship guide him. Exhilaration rushed through him, a sheer joy in speed.

The cliff towered over him.

Luke aimed the ship at the narrow opening of the crevice.

He accelerated, pushing the Podracer as fast as it could go.

And flew straight into the heart of the cliff.

The sunlight disappeared, consumed by darkness as he navigated the narrow, twisting tunnel that wound through the rock. Luke could almost anticipate the turns before they appeared. A sharp right, then two zig-zagging lefts, a hairpin curve around a jagged outcropping.

He'd memorized the map of the course, but he knew that wasn't it.

It was as if he could *feel* the shape of the course, the direction that the Podracer wanted to fly. As if they were alive, and a part of him. He pushed the Podracer even faster, twisting and turning on instinct. A bulky Manta RamAir Podracer, piloted by the cocky Glymphid, appeared ahead of him. Luke shadowed him on the next turn, hugging the inside track. Sparks flew as his engines scraped against the wall of rock — but as they emerged on the straightaway, Luke pulled ahead. As the tunnel released them into open air, Luke passed two of the other racers, shooting ahead toward the next leg of the race.

He turned his face to the wind, jolted by the exhilaration of making it through. Back on Tatooine, he'd raced his T-16 through Beggar's Canyon, secretly imagining it was still part of the famous Mos Espa Podrace circuit. But no amount of imagining could have prepared him for the thrill and terror of an actual race. The deafening rumble of engines. The shuddering vibration of the cockpit, seeping into his bones. The gritty taste of dirt and exhaust fumes in his mouth, as he closed in on the leader, the Bin Gassi Quadrijet. The blur of color and light as the world streaked past.

Unlike the Podraces Luke had seen, this race had only one lap — which meant if he fell behind again, he'd have almost no chance of catching up. According to the map, he would soon reach Aliuun Gorge, a narrow, twisting ravine that tunneled through the earth. It would dead end at the base of a steep plateau, requiring a quick pull up and a near ninety degree climb. From there, he would face a labyrinthine network of underground caves and tunnels that fed into a spiraling vertical passage. If he made it through, it would eventually eject him onto the wide plains for the final straightaway.

The narrow path through the cliff wall had been, by

far, the easiest obstacle he would encounter. Luke squeezed the controls, increasing his thrust. His grip nearly slipped as the Podracer shot forward, bouncing roughly on the Bin Gassi's wake. He felt no fear, only the urge to push harder, to go faster.

A cool certainty flowed through him. He was going to survive.

More than that: He was going to win.

"Unbelievable!" Haari Ikreme Beeerd lowered his electrobinoculars and turned to Han, whom he had apparently decided to forgive in the spirit of the race. "Your human's actually pulling ahead." He shook his lumpy head in confusion. "I never thought he'd make it past the gorge, much less the corckscrew. I've never seen anything like it."

"I have," a grizzled Rodian said. "Though not since that kid back on Tatooine. You're all too young to remember — but I'll never forget. That was something."

"*This* is something," Haari Ikreme countered. He pulled out a stack of credits, muttering to himself. "I wonder if it's too late to change my bet."

The assassin calling himself Tobin Elad peered at the viewscreen, but he was listening intently to the chatter around him. He had assumed his target would be an alien. The piloting skills required to destroy the Death Star were considered beyond human capabilities. Everyone knew that to be true.

But now here was another truth: Luke Skywalker had capabilities like no other human.

"Here they come!" the Rodian shouted, pointing into the distance. Four Podracers appeared on the horizon, screaming toward the finish line.

"He's actually doing it!" Han exclaimed, pounding X-7 on the back.

Luke was pulling up fast on the inside, edging around the Bin Gassi Podracer that had fallen behind after an early lead. The Nuknog at the controls swung a hard left, trying to bump Luke out of the way. Luke weathered the attempt, nudging past the Bin Gassi. The alien veered toward Luke again, too hard, and flung himself into a wild spin. Careening out of control, he nearly crashed into the Vokoff-Strood and the Radon-Ulzer battling it out for the lead. As they struggled to avoid the spiraling Bin Gassi, Luke surged ahead, steering effortlessly around the Nuknog. The cam droids clocked his speed at nearly 850 kilometers per hour.

"He's in the lead!" Han shouted. "I knew the kid had it in him!"

X-7 cloaked his face in a hearty grin.

Is it you? he wondered, watching as Luke's Podracer crossed the finish line, two full seconds ahead of his nearest competitor. *Are you the one I seek?*

If so, Luke's extraordinary piloting skills wouldn't be enough to save him.

You escaped death today, X-7 thought coldly. *But if you're the pilot I'm looking for, you'll never escape me.*

Kenuun's home was nothing like Mak Luunim's. Luunim's apartment had been all gold and silver, loud ostentation that screamed of wealth. Kenuun's apartment, while just as large, was nearly empty. It contained only a few pieces of sleek black furniture, nearly invisible against the black walls. Floor to ceiling transparisteel windows looked down on the Pilaan skyline, and Han realized they must be in one of the tallest buildings in the city. There was wealth here, too, but it was a quiet, careful wealth.

In Han's experience, that was the most powerful kind — and the most dangerous.

"I don't like this," he murmured to Luke and Elad. "We should have insisted on getting the disk at the race. Coming back here feels too risky."

Chewbacca was back at the *Millennium Falcon* with the droids, readying it for take off. As soon as they had the disk in hand, they would be ready to track down Leia and leave this planet behind. It would be a simple, straightforward exchange. If Kenuun followed through with his side of the bargain. Still flush with his unexpected triumph, Luke was acting like they had the mission all wrapped up. But Han's gut was telling him the day was about to become interesting.

And not in a good way.

"Okay, we're here," Han said gruffly. "Now: the datacard."

Kenuun stood on the opposite side of the room, his long arms laced behind his back. "Certainly, but first, won't you sit down? Enjoy a celebratory meal with me? I am, after all, so delighted at our success." If he felt any delight, he was hiding it well. The Muun's face was as stern and expressionless as always.

"We'll just take the datacard and go," Luke said. "As we agreed."

Kenuun nodded. "Of course, of course. Anything for the winning pilot." He tipped his head. "Although, if I could persuade you to stay on, perhaps enter another race —"

"I'll just take the datacard," Luke said.

The Muun nodded again, then pressed a console on the wall. A silk tapestry parted to reveal a silver safe. He thumbed the keypad, and the safe lid opened. Kenuun retrieved a slim datacard, holding it out to Han. "I believe this is what you've been looking for?"

Han inserted the datacard into his datapad and confirmed it. The Muun had upheld his side of the bargain after all. "Pleasure doing business with you, Nal."

"And you as well," the Muun said slowly. "*Captain Solo*."

Han froze. He'd never given the Muun his real identity. None of them had.

"Oh yes," Nal Kenuun said. *Now* he smiled. "I know who you are. All of you." He signaled with a spindly finger, and four stormtroopers emerged from hidden niches in the wall. They positioned themselves around the room, one in each corner, blasters aimed. "There's a bounty on your head, Captain Solo — and yours, too, Tobin Elad. I expect that should be enough to repay me what I'm owed. With interest."

"We owe you nothing," Han snarled.

"Not you," the Muun said coolly. "The boy." He narrowed his eyes at Luke. "That was a rather valuable vehicle you destroyed in your 'practice' session."

Luke's eyes widened. "It was defective!"

"Be that as it may, the Podracer was intact when it left my possession," Kenuun said. "Now it's a heap of desert rubble. And as you know, debts must be repaid."

"So let *me* pay," Luke said defiantly. "I'm the one who crashed it. Let the rest of them go, I'll stay here —"

"Luke!" Han protested.

"*I'll stay*," Luke said loudly, over Han's objections. "I'll win another race for you."

"Yes, you *will* stay. And you will certainly race again." Kenuun nodded slowly. "But next time, you may not survive. Leaving the debt unpaid. A bounty, on the other hand, is certain to line my pockets with credits. I may be a gambler when it suits me — but it's not the way of the Muun to pass up opportunities for sure financial gain."

"I thought it wasn't the way of the Muun to break contracts," Han pointed out. "We had a deal." He jerked a thumb at Luke. "The kid here put his life on the line for you."

Kenuun flashed a cruel smile. "Our agreement was for the boy's services, in return for your disk. Which, as you may have noticed, you now have in your possession. The terms of our contract included nothing about what was to happen once our exchange was concluded. I never offered you safe passage off the planet, or off my property."

"You do have a point," Han said, stalling as he tried furiously to think of a plan.

"And I do have a rather large bounty on my head," Elad added.

"Nothing compared to mine, I'm sure," Han said.

"I wouldn't be *too* sure — I'm a dangerous man," Elad countered.

"Yeah?" Han whipped out his blaster and shot down the nearest guard. "Prove it!"

But Elad was already in motion, a sharp kick sweeping the legs out from one of the stormtroopers while he simultaneously fired at another one on the opposite side of the room.

Luke dodged a barrage of fire, diving over a couch. He swore as one of the guards shot the blaster out of his hand, then activated his lightsaber, lashing out with the glowing beam. The stormtrooper darted out of his reach, then fired again. Luke grunted in pain and toppled backward as the laserfire blasted into his shoulder.

Han rushed to help — then stopped, as he felt something sharp jab him in the back.

"Drop it," the guard's flat voice ordered.

Han raised his arms, letting his blaster clatter to the floor. Luke groaned and sat up — but a blaster in the face stopped him from going any further. The other two stormtroopers lay on the ground, unconscious or dead. Han grimaced — they'd almost managed to win.

But when blasters were involved, almost didn't count.

"Why don't *you* drop it," Elad suggested in a dry voice.

Han craned his neck around to see Elad standing at

the entrance of the room, his blaster pressed against Nal Kenuun's narrow head.

"You shoot them, I'll shoot your boss," Elad warned.

The Muun appeared unfazed. "We seem to be at an impasse," he said serenely. "What do you propose?"

"How about you let us walk out of here, and we don't shoot you where you stand," Han growled.

"I hardly think *you're* in a position to be making offers," Kenuun said. In case his point wasn't clear, the stormtrooper jabbed Han with the blaster again. Hard.

"I propose a trade," Elad said. "Let them go free, and I'll remain here as your prisoner. The boy's worth nothing to you, and the bounty on Han is negligible compared to mine."

"Negligible?" Han asked incredulously. "There's nothing negligible about the amount that Jabba wants me dead. Trust me."

"You speak the truth," the Muun told Elad. "And your offer interests me."

"Can we go back to the negligible thing?" Han persisted. "Half the bounty hunters in the galaxy are after me! I don't know who this guy is or what he did, but when it comes to rewards, I'm the one you want, trust me."

Kenuun ignored him. "You will sacrifice your weapon and remain here peaceably until I turn you in for a reward?"

Elad nodded. "But *only* if you guarantee the *Millennium Falcon* — its *entire* crew — safe passage off planet. No more technicalities or loopholes this time."

"Elad, you can't do this!" Luke protested, rising to his feet. The guard's blaster stayed trained on him.

"It's like you said, Luke. Some things are more important than an individual life. Of course, I didn't intend for the life in question to be mine, but . . ." Elad smiled grimly. "Fortunately, there's no one left to mourn the loss."

The Muun made his decision. "I accept your offer, Tobin Elad. You have a deal."

"I think we still need to negotiate some of the finer points," Leia said, stepping into the room, her blaster at the ready. In her other hand, she held an odd length of rope, tethered to something hidden behind the doorframe.

"Leia?" Han said in disbelief. "What are *you* doing here?"

Leia raised her eyebrows. "You didn't actually expect the Muun to keep his word, did you? We figured a backup plan might be in order."

Han scowled at the princess. Why did she always insist on putting herself in danger? "Funny, last I checked, *we* included *me*."

"Well, this time, it included *Luke*," she said, smirking.

"You were busy. Something about a fistfight with a loud-mouthed Phlog?"

"I hate to interrupt," Kenuun said coldly, "but I fail to see how this trespasser's appearance affects the equation. Unless perhaps she'd like to offer herself up as a sacrifice as well?"

"Thought about that," Leia said. "But then I came up with a better idea." She stepped farther into the room, revealing that the rope she held was actually a leash. It was attached to a golden collar, fastened around the neck of a slobbering krayt dragon, measuring less than a meter from its sharp horns to the tip of its spiny tail. Its forked tongue flickered around its yellowish lips.

"Urgiluu!" the Muun cried, exhibiting the first real sign of alarm. "What have you done to her?"

"Nothing." Leia lowered the tip of her blaster until it was aimed at the dragon's scaly face. "Yet."

"You must be *careful*," the Muun urged. "The pearl forming inside her is *extremely* delicate — and any malformations would significantly detract from its value."

"*That's* why you're such a softie about the dragon?" Han asked in disgust. "Because it can make you money?"

"What other possible value could any creature have?" the Muun asked disdainfully.

"Not everything's about money," Han said. Leia glanced sharply at him, surprise in her eyes. *So that's what she really thinks of me*, Han realized. *She thinks I'm like* him.

"Not everything," Kenuun agreed. "Just everything that matters." Still, there was no denying the concern in his eyes as he tracked the tip of Leia's blaster. Whatever the reason, he wanted that dragon to remain intact.

Kenuun hesitated.

"Drop your weapons," he said finally. "You may go." As swiftly and silently as the guards appeared, they vanished. He held out his hand to Leia. "The leash, if you please?"

"You will accompany us back to our ship," Leia said in an imperious tone. It was suddenly easy for Han to imagine her on the floor of the Galactic Senate. "When we are ready to take off, then and only then, will I return your property."

"But I *guarantee* your safe passage off the planet and out of the atmosphere," the Muun pleaded, his fingers clutching compulsively as if gripping an invisible leash. He struggled to retain his dignity, even while begging. "I am a *Muun*, after all. That should be guarantee enough that I will keep my word."

"Maybe it should be," Leia said, tugging on the leash so the krayt dragon was forced to heel. "But it's not."

CHAPTER TWENTY TWO

You weren't *actually* going to kill that helpless little dragon, were you?" Luke asked, grinning. The *Falcon* had just made the jump to hyperspace. Now that the Rebellion's financial codes were safely in hand and Muun was dropping further away by the second, everyone was in good spirits.

"Helpless?" Han snorted. "Tell that to the last guy I know who tangled with a krayt dragon. Might be a kind of one-sided conversation though, seeing as how he ended up in pieces."

"I figured Kenuun would give in," Leia said with more than a hint of pride. "I only snuck in there to provide you with some backup, if you needed it — but when I spotted the dragon, I remembered what Han heard from the Podracers. Negotiation seemed like a somewhat better option than blasting our way out."

"Ah ha!" Han said triumphantly. "So the truth comes out. Lucky thing I went into that tent, or I wouldn't have been able to provide the crucial information."

"Lucky thing you came out of that tent alive," Leia retorted, "given the way you were acting."

"What about you?" Han shot back. "Sneaking into Kenuun's place like that."

"And *I* still can't believe you didn't realize Luke and I staged that argument for Kenuun's benefit. You really think I would pick a fight with him before he was about to risk his *life*?"

Han glared at her. "I *thought* we were a team. Which means when you come up with some insane plan, you fill me in."

"Oh, you would've been all for it?"

"I would've told you it was crazy! I never would have let you do something like that."

"Exactly why I didn't tell you."

"You want to know your problem, princess?" Han asked.

Leia leaned forward. "Amaze me."

"You don't think before you act."

"*I* don't think?" she asked incredulously.

"That's right." He stretched out in his chair, suddenly enjoying himself. "You don't think, and so you get yourself into these crazy situations, and I've got to come in and rescue you."

"*You've* got to rescue *me?*" Leia said. She stood up. "Chewbacca!" she shouted down the corridor. "Chewbacca, get up here!"

"What do you want with him?" Han asked.

"I want him to turn this ship around and head straight back to Muun, you egotistical, nerf-brained buffoon!" Leia snapped. "We'll drop you off at Kenuun's place, and you can see how well you do without *me* there to rescue *you.*"

"Yeah, Chewie, get up here!" Han shouted. "Tell *Her Highness* that her rescuing me *once* doesn't cancel out the twenty times I've risked my neck to rescue her."

"And you can tell this Kowakian monkey-lizard that no one asked him to!" Leia shouted, even louder.

But instead of the Wookiee, Elad appeared in the doorway. "I didn't mean to interrupt," he said politely. "I was just looking for Luke. That is, if you're still interested in doing some hand-to-hand combat training."

"Of course!" Luke said eagerly.

Han suspected he was just happy for an excuse to escape all the bickering. Han couldn't blame him. But he couldn't force himself to stop — not if it meant letting Leia get the last word.

"Luke, wait." Leia stood up. "I need to talk to Elad for a moment. If that's all right with him, of course."

"Of course," Elad said. "Consider me at your service."

We were *in the middle of something*, Han thought irritably, as Leia and Elad left the cockpit. Nothing important, of course. Nothing they couldn't argue about later.

But he couldn't help wondering what she wanted to talk to Elad about — in private.

I'm sure it's nothing important, he told himself. Not that he cared.

Not at all.

"I want to apologize," Leia said, once they were alone in her quarters.

Elad looked confused. "For what?"

Leia hesitated. Apologies didn't come easily to her. And there was nothing she disliked more than being proven wrong. "For not trusting you," Leia admitted. "You put yourself in danger for us — for the Rebellion — again and again. I should have seen that your motives were pure."

"You're wise to be cautious," Elad assured her. "I would feel the same."

Leia shook her head. "I heard what you said to Kenuun. You were willing to give your life to save Han and Luke. Near strangers."

"Not for them," Elad corrected her. "For the Rebellion. They can be more valuable to the cause than

I can — and, as I told you, this the only cause I have. Fighting the Empire is my only reason to go on."

"Then join us!" Leia said. It wasn't an impulse. She'd been thinking about this for days. Elad was exactly the kind of man they needed in the Rebellion: Smart, brave, loyal.

Like Han could be, she thought sadly. *If he ever stops running from who he really is.*

"I don't know," Elad said. "I'm pretty used to going it alone. The idea of being part of something again . . ." He shook his head. "Letting people into your life always seems like a good idea at the start. But it can end . . . badly."

Leia knew what he was referring to. Her heart clenched. "Just think about it," she said softly, putting a hand on his shoulder. "You can't lock yourself away from the world forever." She hadn't touched him since the first day they'd spoken. Since then, she had barely trusted herself to speak to him. She hadn't wanted to risk opening herself up again. Whenever she looked in his eyes, all she could see was the pain of her own losses reflected back at her. But now, for the first time, she didn't look away. "You're better off for having known your wife and your child," she said hesitantly, unsure of whether she was crossing an invisible line. "The time you shared with them is worth suffering the pain of their absence."

Elad jerked away from her. "You can't know that."

"I can," Leia drew a deep, shuddering breath. Maybe it was time to take her own advice. She'd kept her feelings — her pain — locked up for so long. Maybe just saying the words out loud, just telling *someone* about what she had lost, maybe that would help salve the wound. "I can know, because . . . because of Alderaan."

Her voice caught on the word.

Elad's expression didn't change. It was as if he'd known this moment would arrive. "Do you want to talk about it?"

She had already decided on her answer, but was surprised to find how deeply she meant it. "Yes."

X-7 confirmed that his encrypted communication line was secure, then activated the transmission. The others were all in the main hold, so there was no risk anyone would overhear.

"I've gained the trust of the Rebels," he informed the Commander. It was a relief to drop the hearty heroism of the Elad persona and relax into the blankness of his true self. "The goal is close at hand."

"Excellent," the Commander replied. "I expect you to secure the information about our target as soon as possible. Time is of the essence."

"I may already have a lead."

"Keep me informed," the Commander said, and signed off.

X-7 decided to join the others in the main hold. No need to sequester himself anymore, now that their leader had accepted him.

More than accepted him, he thought with cool pleasure. Sought comfort in him. Friendship. He had done well in his formulation of the Tobin Elad identity. As predicted, the wounded, noble warrior was exactly the person Leia wanted in her life. Even if she hadn't realized it until "Elad" appeared.

These humans were all so trusting, X-7 thought in disgust. So eager to believe in what they saw on the surface. They believed in the bond that drew them together. They thought it made them strong. And maybe it did. But their secrets kept them apart.

And that made them weak.

They may have fancied themselves as cautious, but it was a joke. They looked at X-7 and saw what they wanted to see — what *he* wanted them to see.

For Han, he would be a brother in arms. The bounty had been a nice touch, X-7 thought, congratulating himself on constructing such a thorough false identity. Kenuun had done him a true service by digging into "Elad's" records. There could surely be no faster way of gaining Han's trust.

For Leia, he would be her equal, the bold warrior as committed to the fight as she was. He would be what she wished Han Solo could be — a secret she hid even from herself.

But there were no secrets from X-7.

For Luke? For Luke, he would be a confidante, the one man who believed he would achieve his Jedi destiny.

And this was no act: X-7 believed. He had seen Luke pilot that Podracer — he knew what the boy was capable of. And if Luke was his target, well . . . a Jedi Knight would make a formidable adversary. But by his own admission, Luke was no Jedi. Not yet.

X-7 stood silently at the edge of the main hold, unobserved. Observing.

Watching as Leia and Han peered at a datapad, bickering loudly over its contents.

Watching as the Wookiee played a game of dejarik with the golden protocol droid, growling whenever it fell behind.

Watching as Luke — expert pilot, aspiring Jedi, possibly the Rebellion's great hope — fumbled with his lightsaber. The blue beam flashed as he struggled to deflect shots fired by the astromech droid, missing one after another. A moment later, he stumbled over his own feet, toppling backward and landing on the floor in a heap.

X-7 rarely experienced emotions. But thinking of these pathetic humans believing they were a match for any of their enemies — much less an enemy like him — X-7 allowed himself a genuine smile.

This is going to be even easier than I thought.